"GENA, WHAT'S GOING ON? WHY WOULD SOMEONE BE TRYING TO KILL YOU?"

Rik pulled Gena close and walked her into the motel room. He shut the door.

"Why are you questioning me like this?" she asked.

"You offered me a lot of money when I was in jail."

"So?"

"Where did you get that kinda money?"

She turned and headed for the door. Rik grabbed her.

"Gena, did you find Qua's money?"

"Rik, let me go! What the hell is wrong with you?"

He backhanded her. Gena stumbled back a few steps, and then raced for the door. She was able to snatch it open before he grabbed her.

"Help me!" Gena screamed. "Somebody help me!"

"Shut up and just tell me where the rest of the money is," Rik shouted. He slung Gena onto the bed, then tried to kick the motel door closed. The door flew back open. Someone she knew was standing in the doorway . . .

"Four out of five . . . Wonderful . . . a great story . . . a fast-paced exciting read that will surely keep you on your toes."
—Urban-Reviews.com on *True to the Game II*

TERI WOODS

TRUE
TO THE
GAME
III

GRAND CENTRAL
PUBLISHING

NEW YORK   BOSTON

Grand Central Publishing
Hachette Book Group USA
237 Park Avenue
New York, NY 10017

Visit our Web site at www.HachetteBookGroupUSA.com.

Printed in the United States of America

First Edition: July 2008
10 9 8 7 6 5

Grand Central Publishing is a division of Hachette Book Group USA, Inc.
The Grand Central Publishing name and logo is a trademark of Hachette Book Group USA, Inc.

Library of Congress Cataloging-in-Publication Data

Woods, Teri.
  True to the game III / Teri Woods. — 1st ed.
    p. cm.
  Summary: "In this ending to a trilogy, Gena struggles with being able to finally let go of Quadir in order to make a life for herself. But when past demons catch up with her, Gena's life is on the line as she tries to protect the only family she has left"—Provided by the publisher.
  ISBN: 978-0-446-58168-4
  1. African Americans—Fiction. 2. Drug dealers—Fiction. 3. Philadelphia (Pa.)—Fiction.
I. Title. II. Title: True to the game three.
  PS3573.O6427T79 2008
  813'.54—dc22

                                                                    2007039788

This book is dedicated to
Leon Blue

ACKNOWLEDGMENTS

Mom, Corel, Jessica, Chuck, Dexter, Carl, Brenda,
Lucas, Brandon, and my girlfriend, Kashan.
Oh yeah, my secretary, Tracy.

Thanks.

TRUE
TO THE
GAME
III

PROLOGUE

February 18, 1991

Gena slowly tried to open her eyes, feeling pain beyond belief throughout her entire body. She was bruised from her head to her toes. She looked around the room, not quite realizing where she was. At first, she had thought she was in a hospital, lying in a bed. But, as time passed, she realized she wasn't. The room's décor was unlike any hospital décor that she had ever seen. Her head, left arm, rib cage, and left thigh were all bandaged. She could barely open her bruised and blackened eyes. She couldn't pull herself out of the bed without feeling agonizing pain. Her body felt sore and she needed rest. Her only assurance that she was safe was that she was being taken care of by a nurse and a doctor. She felt the nurse near her bedside constantly and could overhear the nurse talking to the doctor in the distance. She sang to her, she read to her, and she talked to her. The kind and loving nurse fed Gena and gave her pain medication and sleeping pills. She closed her eyes again.

Gena rested her body and mustered her strength as the weeks

passed. Early one morning, Gena awoke to a ruckus outside her bedroom door. The sound of voices filled the tiny hallway. Startled but not afraid, Gena looked around the room. It was intricately designed, with a touch of sophistication; Gena did not recognize anything. *Where am I?* She couldn't help but begin to wonder. She decided to make finding the answer to that question her life's mission. Ready to move around, Gena rose from the king-size bed that she had been lying on. There was a breeze blowing through an open window, she noticed, as the soft silk panels were billowing gently with the air. She could smell the sweet fragrance of flowers wafting through the window. She mustered up as much strength as she could, desperately wanting to know where she was.

Gena clasped one of the bedposts and made her way to the bottom of the four-poster bed. From there she threw her wobbly legs forward and grabbed hold of a nearby accent chair. She braced herself using the arms of the chair, and then carefully made her way around it, until she was able to grab onto a nearby dresser. Using the dresser as a support, she slowly made her way to the open window, where she was finally able to peer outside and get a glimpse of her surroundings.

She was on the second floor of what appeared to be a home. She could see very large homes all around her. Steeply pitched slate- and granite-tiled roofs and well-manicured backyards with massive swimming pools and tennis courts filled her view. She peered down into the backyard just below her and found an equally large swimming pool and adjacent tennis court, along with the fragrant garden that had attracted her attention initially. The azaleas, roses, Russian sage, gardenias, and other flora spread throughout the landscape painted it in rich hues of blue, red, white, yellow, green, and purple. *Where the hell am I?*

Gena turned toward the dresser and pulled open the first drawer, only to find it empty. She moved on to the second drawer, to find it in the same state. The third, fourth, fifth, and sixth dresser drawers were also empty. She was in a guest bedroom, and there were no secrets kept here. She turned and spied two doors on the opposite side of the room. One she surmised to be a closet, while the other would have to be the guest bathroom. Hoping that the closet or the medicine cabinet would reveal something, she made her way across the room toward them. She had regained her equilibrium and was doing quite well moving around the room.

Gena opened the first door to find a row of plastic clothes hangers facing her. There was nothing on the shelves, nothing stored at the bottom of the closet, nothing period. Disappointed, she turned her attention to the next door. She had been correct in her assumptions, as the second door was to the guest bathroom. Gena braced herself on the door handle and stumbled inside. She held on to the bathroom sink and yanked open the medicine cabinet. Nothing.

"Dammit!" Gena cursed. She was growing frustrated with each passing moment. She was in a luxurious prison, all alone and wounded. She couldn't run away if she tried. Her entire body was one big ache and pain. *Think, Gena,* she told herself. *Think. What do you remember? What do you remember?*

Gena thought long and hard as she slowly made her way back to the massive four-poster bed, where she lay down again. *Where am I and who brought me here?* She started to think back and remembered Jerrell. *We were in a motel.* It was then she remembered going into the bathroom and looking in the duffel bag Jerrell had under the sink. She remembered the duffel bag full of money, and the rope, the bottle of acid, buckets of cement, the metal handcuffs, and chains. Jerrell had taken her to a motel room where he had tried to kill her. She remembered fighting him. *Yes, I remember, but then what? What happened? Did I trip or fall or something? No, I was running for the door when he grabbed me, and then . . . ?* At first Gena could not recall, then she slowly began to remember. *The gun. Someone shot Jerrell and saved me, or was it Jerrell who fired the gun?*

Who had done the shooting and who got shot? *Did Jerrell shoot someone? He was trying to kill me and now he must have me here, holding me hostage. What the hell does he think he's doing? It doesn't even make sense. If he was going to kill me, why didn't he just go ahead and do it? Someone else must have saved me, but who? None of this makes any sense at all.*

Nothing added up. She was bandaged but had no idea who had treated her wounds. She was somewhere, but didn't have a clue where, and she was definitely in someone's house, but again, had no idea whose. She had been in and out of consciousness, but had no idea for how long. *Someone's obviously been taking care of me,* she thought. Someone had bandaged her up, given her medicine, fed her, and kept her clean. Someone had expended a lot of effort to heal her and care for her. *But who?*

Gena leaned back and closed her eyes, and her tears began to fall. Her mind had granted her an additional memory from that night, one that she knew could not be true. She had dreamed that Quadir was alive. She was barely conscious, but it all seemed so real at the time. Her Quadir had rescued her from that monster, and carried her off to safety. *If only it could be true.*

Gena clutched her stomach and curled into a ball on the bed. It was then that she remembered the visit with her OB/GYN.

"Congratulations, you're going to have a baby," Dr. Amerson said joyfully, smiling from ear to ear at the other end of the examining table.

A baby, my baby. She couldn't help but think of the unborn child she was carrying as she rubbed her belly. She was in a dire predicament. *That's right, I was going to tell him about the baby,* she thought to herself, remembering how nervous she was and how she couldn't wait to hear what he would say. She had been hoping that Jerrell would be pleased with her and happy for the both of them. She was so ready to be with him and be a family. *How could I have been so dumb? He didn't love me; he didn't even care about me. He was trying to kill me.* Gena couldn't believe it. She was carrying the child of a man who had tried to kill her, fantasizing about a man who had been dead now for almost a year. *I can't believe Jerrell has me here. It's only a matter of time before he comes back to finish me off. My only chance will be to try to escape, go get my money, and get out of town. That's what Jerrell wanted: Quadir's money. He never wanted to be with me. He could have cared less.* That reality brought a tear to Gena's eye and she realized at that moment that Jerrell had only been pretending to love and care about her. *How was I so stupid that I didn't see him for what he really was? I can't believe he was after my money.* Gena just sat on the edge of the bed thinking about everything that had happened, unable to justify anything and unwilling to believe that it was all happening to her. *I wonder where he is. Shit, where the hell am I? And how long have I been here?* She needed to get in touch with Gah Git. She needed to talk to her grandmother and tell her where she was and let her know that she was all right. Gah Git would be worried half to death. *Poor Gah Git. I hope she's okay.* Gena had already looked around the room and there was no phone. *Someone has to help me; I need to be rescued. But rescued from who? Whoever it is that bandaged my wounds, fed me, and took care of me? Yes, I definitely need to be rescued, especially if that person is Jerrell.*

The door to the room cracked open and Gena expected the worse. Instead, she was greeted by a plump and friendly housekeeper.

"Oh, my God! Señorita, you're awake!" the housekeeper said. "Oh, they will be so pleased! Mr. Smith is about to have breakfast on the lanai. I can bring your breakfast out there so that you can eat with him. He will be so pleased, señorita! It is so good to see that you are awake now!"

"Who are you? And who is Mr. Smith?" Gena asked.

"My name is Consuela, and Mr. Smith is Señorita Hopkins's boyfriend," the housekeeper explained. "Señor Smith is the one who rescued you and brought you here."

"Rescued me?" Gena was confused. She shook her head to rid herself of the cobwebs inside. *Who is Mr. Smith?* Gena needed to see this Mr. Smith. She needed to talk to him and she needed him to fill in all the blanks from that night. What had happened? Where was Jerrell? Why did Mr. Smith bring her here? She had a million and one questions that needed answering.

Gena began to rise. Consuela rushed to her and helped her stand.

"No, wait here," Consuela told her. "Señorita Hopkins

brought something for you, just for when this day would come."

Consuela rushed out of the room and returned seconds later with a metal walker. She placed the walker in front of Gena and then clasped her arm.

"I'll help you to the elevator and then to the porch. I'll bring your breakfast out to the garden."

"Thank you so much. But I can walk," Gena told her.

"Are you sure?" said Consuela as if it were a miracle.

"Yes, yes, of course. You are very kind, though. Thank you, but I'm fine, I can walk."

"*Ven*, I will help you."

Consuela helped Gena to the elevator, and they rode it to the first floor. The doors to the elevator opened, revealing a massive two-story family room. The dimensions made Gena gasp.

The room was forty by sixty, with a ten-foot-diameter wrought-iron chandelier. Antique furnishings and expensive décor filled the room. The art and tapestries that hung on the wall were all original, while the tables all looked to be hand carved with great care and detail.

"Who lives here?" Gena asked.

"Señorita Hopkins," Consuela told her. "She is at work right now. Señor Smith is out on the lanai."

Gena followed as Consuela led her across the living room, out of the large double patio doors, and onto the lanai. A gentleman was seated across the lanai, facing away from them, looking over the swimming pool. She could see that he was dressed all in white and reading a newspaper. A table with a pitcher of orange juice was next to him, and she could see that he had already poured a glass.

"Señor Smith," Consuela called out to him. "Look who has awakened."

Gena watched as the stranger rose from the chair and turned to her. Consuela had to catch her.

"Señorita, are you all right?" Consuela asked.

It can't be. It can't be. Gena shook her head.

"I'll take it from here," he told Consuela.

"No. No. It's not possible. I don't understand. You're dead!" Gena said, staring at a ghost.

He guided her to a nearby table and poured her a glass of water.

"You're alive," Gena said softly. She gently caressed his face, reassuring herself that she was not dreaming. "You're alive!" Tears streamed from her eyes as she covered her face. Quadir sat next to her and gently placed his arm around her.

"Gena, it's okay. I'm here now."

He kissed her face and took her hand in his, and rubbed it gently against his face. He was alive. Her Qua was here with her, and he was alive! *But how?* was the only thing she could think. She looked over at him; sure as day he was there. *How could this miracle be possible? I saw him dead at the hospital. I was at his funeral.* Gena sat still in silence. Neither of the two said a word. Quadir didn't want to interrupt her thoughts, and he knew his presence was just as heavy as his death. He had done what he had to do and what was best for him at that time, but he had never meant to hurt her. Confused, Gena didn't know what to say next.

"I don't understand."

She looked him in the eyes for a split second and wondered if he had any idea what he had put her through. Out of nowhere, she slapped his face once and watched his blank expression. She started to slap him again, but he caught her hand and held it in his.

"Why you beatin' on me?" he asked with a smile.

"Why are you alive? You're supposed to be dead."

She shoved him away, and a frown shot across her face. "Where have you been? How could you do that to me? How could you be alive? I don't understand. I saw you; you were dead."

Quadir nodded. "I know, Gena, I know. I have a lot of explaining to do."

"You're goddamned right you do! How could you let me think that you were dead? How could you just up and leave me like that, without telling me anything? Do you know the hell that I've been through since you died? Do you?"

Gena tried to slap him again, and again he caught her wrist and prevented her from hitting him.

"You bastard! You're an asshole! You sorry, inconsiderate son of a bitch!"

"Gena, wait!" Quadir held her down. "Calm down! You're going to bust your stitches. You have to take it easy until you have fully recovered. I'll explain everything. I promise. Just give me a chance."

"What possible explanation could you have for what you have done to me? To us? Why would you put me through all of that?"

"I had to. I had no choice. I had people trying to kill me and the police about to indict me. I just needed to start over. And I needed for it to look real."

"So you had someone kill you? I was there that night. I saw you die."

"No, that part was real," Quadir explained. "I had nothing

to do with them sorry-ass Junior Mafia motherfuckers shooting at us. Are you crazy? They really tried to kill me. In fact, they did. All of that was real, baby. But, once I got to the hospital, I was resuscitated. I can't explain it; I just wouldn't let go. There was something inside of me like a light that refused to go out. That light was my love for you, Gena. My love for you wouldn't let me die," he said, hoping kind and submissive words would appeal to her ego.

"Nigga, is you crazy? You was dead. I seen you; you was dead." Gena recrossed her arms and lifted a questioning eyebrow. "If you weren't dead, why didn't you call me, Quadir? Why didn't anyone call me and let me know that you were alive? Do you know how crazy you sound right now?"

"Because, baby, everyone thought that I was dead. That was the only way my plan would work. It was my only chance to get away from the police and from the Junior Mafia. I was going to go down South, Gena. I was going to get everything set up, and then I was going to come for you."

"And why couldn't I be a part of the plan? Why couldn't you have let me know what was going on?"

"Because I needed my death to be real and I knew you were the biggest key to everyone believing I was gone. I needed to let everything die down first, and I needed you to convince everyone that I was dead and buried."

"Who did I bury?"

Quadir exhaled. He released Gena, took a seat on the wicker sofa across from hers, and settled in for the long story that he was about to tell her. "You may want to eat a little something before I get started."

"Quadir, I will die of starvation before I let either of us leave this lanai and I still be in the dark," Gena told him. "I hope that this little explanation of yours is a good one. If it's not, I'm going to kill you myself. And this time, there won't be no coming back."

Quadir smiled and leaned back on the sofa. "It's like this . . ."

HEAVEN CAN WAIT

Hahnemann Hospital, January 1, 1990

The orderly strolled into the room to collect his cadaver. He had been at the job for a little more than a year now, and he loved it. Working in the hospital morgue paid well and afforded him the peace and quiet that he needed to study for his premed courses. The job suited him more than most, as his goal was to become a surgeon. He was now in his final year of premed, and one semester away from actual medical school, where he would be cutting open bodies and not just transporting them from one floor to another.

The body that he was picking up now was fresh. The gunshot victim had just been called, and his family had just walked out of the room. *Probably the guy's wife or fiancée or something, but whoever she was, she certainly had a nice little ass on her. This poor, unlucky bastard would now be staring down or up, watching somebody else plow that fat-ass onion she had back there.*

The orderly lifted the cadaver's hanging hand to lay it on the bed. The hand felt weird. Stranger than any other dead guy's hand he had ever touched. The damn thing was warm, really warm. And more than that, it had a fucking pulse.

"Oh, shit!" The orderly rushed into the hall to find a nurse, a doctor, anyone who looked like they could do something. "Excuse me, ma'am. I have an emergency."

Dr. Hopkins stopped and read the orderly's name tag. "Stan, what can I do for you?"

"Doc, I got a dead guy in there who ain't dead," Stan told her.

"What?" Dr. Hopkins rushed into the emergency operating room. She clasped Quadir's pulse. Sure as shit, he had one. She rushed to the wall and pressed the intercom.

"Stat. Emergency room personnel to the OR, stat. This is Dr. Amelia Hopkins. Emergency room surgical personnel to the OR, immediately!"

Masked emergency room personnel ran into the operating room, some of them still covered with Quadir's blood from minutes ago.

"We got a live one here, people!" Dr. Hopkins shouted. She rushed to a corner of the room to scrub up before several nurses dressed her in surgical garb. Two more surgeons, Dr. Benjamin Brant and Dr. William Hartley, rushed into the room. "Ben, he's still alive."

"Hot damn!" Dr. Brant rushed to Quadir and immediately began working on him.

Dr. Hartley began issuing orders as he scrubbed up and the nurses dressed him in surgical garb.

"You're a tough son of a bitch, aren't you?" Dr. Brant said, smiling at Quadir. "Fight, son. That's right, fight."

"Set up a pint of plasma for him." Hopkins ordered one of

the nurses. "Get him hooked back up so that we can monitor his blood pressure. What's the deal, Benny?"

"Couldn't find that last fucking bullet. It hid behind his heart. He flatlined and we couldn't get him back. We called him."

"You need a woman's touch in here," Hopkins told him. "My hands are a lot smaller than yours. Let me see if I can work my way around in there and get that little booger."

Dr. Brant maneuvered out of the way and allowed Dr. Hopkins to become the primary surgeon. Within seconds she was smiling at him beneath her surgical mask.

"Was this the pesky little thing you were looking for?" she asked, holding up a small, bloody, lead ball. She placed the bullet into a small dish, and then proceeded to repair the internal damage it had caused.

"Ben and I repaired most of the damage already," Hartley told her.

"I see; you guys did a fantastic job," she told him, assuaging their egos. Dr. Hopkins reconnected a severed artery, suctioned the blood from the wound, and monitored her patient for several moments before turning to a nurse. "What's he looking like?"

"Blood pressure has climbed to 112 over 70 and is holding steady. Everything looks good."

"Close him up for me, get him into ICU, and page me in an hour with his vitals," Hopkins told them. She lifted the chart from the bottom of the bed. "Deceased" had been scrawled across it. "Get him a new chart. The patient's name is John Smith. Everybody clear on that?"

Dr. Brant peered over at his colleague.

"I'll alert the authorities and his family," Dr. Hopkins told them. "Until I or the authorities say otherwise, Mr. Richards is deceased. Mr. Smith, however, is alive and doing quite well."

"I signed the death certificate," Hartley told her.

"I'll take care of that, too," Hopkins said. She turned to the orderly, who had watched the whole thing from the corner of the operating room. "Come with me."

Amelia Hopkins led Stan out into the hallway and maneuvered him into a corner. "Stan, what I am about to say to you is very important. And I need to have your undivided attention. Do I have that, Stan? Do I have your undivided attention?"

Stan nodded. "Yes, ma'am."

"Good. Stan, I have a patient in there who had a whole lot of bullet holes inside of him. Somebody doesn't like Mr. Richards, and thought it best that he not remain with us in this life. My job, as a doctor, is to see to it that he does. But in order to do that, I am going to need your help. Can I count on you to help me?"

Stan nodded again.

"Good. Now, how many John Does do you have down there in the morgue?"

"Right now, about four or five, but the weekend is coming up. We should have a shitload of 'em coming in."

Amelia Hopkins nodded. "Any of the ones we have fit the description of Mr. Richards in there?"

Stan smiled and scratched his chin. "One, maybe. A buddy of mines works over in the morgue at the County Hospital. I'm sure I could get you a John Doe close enough to match."

It was Dr. Hopkins's turn to smile. "You do that. You get me a John Doe to match, and you put this chart on him. Make sure that John Doe becomes Quadir Richards. And you let no one in to see it. He's already been identified by his family, and you tell them that the authorities are not allowing anyone else to see the body at this time. You got that?"

Stan nodded. "Dr. Hopkins, in a few years, I'll need a surgeon to intern under."

Amelia shoved the chart into his hand. "You want to be a surgeon, I'll get you there. But you better have the grades and the stamina to keep up with me."

Stan nodded. "Deal."

Dr. Hopkins walked to the nurses' station. "That patient in the OR. I need for you to get me his family's address and telephone number. You'll probably have to look it up. You know what, see if you can cross-reference the information that you find and get me the name and telephone number of his parents."

The nurse nodded and lifted a large telephone book from beneath the nurses' station.

Dr. Hopkins knew that one thing was for certain: a mother would do anything to keep her child alive. A wife or girlfriend could be after an insurance policy, or her jealous lover could have been the gunman. But a mother, she would kill or die to protect her offspring. She needed the mother's address.

The nurses and a couple of ICU orderlies wheeled Quadir out of the operating room, heading for the elevator.

"What's he look like?" Hopkins asked.

"Vitals are stable. Blood pressure is 118 over 80."

"Good job, Amelia," Dr. Brant told her, exiting the operating room.

"Thanks, Benny."

"I'm heading over to the cafeteria. Want to join me?" Dr. Brant asked.

Amelia nodded. She could use something to eat. Besides,

she wanted to run a few things by Dr. Brant. He was her mentor, and she trusted him completely. It had been Dr. Brant who had trained her and helped her to hone her surgical skills to what they were today. Benny Brant was probably one of the top surgeons in the country. And for him, a wealthy Jewish surgeon from New York, to have taken a poor black girl from the Alabama countryside under his wing was unfathomable. He had dozens of doctors from some of the finest families all over the country trying to intern under him, some of whom where the sons of his colleagues. The fact that he had pulled her under his wing was something that she would forever be grateful for.

The two of them headed for the elevator.

GAME PLAN

Amelia moved through the parking garage with the ferocity of a cheetah on the prowl. Her determined steps took her rapidly through the parking structure to the secluded corner where her meeting was to take place. The person with whom she was to meet was already there.

"Viola Richards?" she asked.

Viola nodded. "What's going on? Why did you ask for me to meet you here?"

Amelia peered around the parking garage to make sure they were alone. Still, she thought it best that they move to the even more secluded second level. She clasped Viola's arm and led her off.

"I wanted to meet you here because I had some questions about your son. I operated on him in the emergency room."

Viola sniffled. "Do the police have any suspects or leads in the case?" she asked, shaking her head. "You know how they are. My son was a young black man whose occupation was questionable. In situations like these, they don't care about finding the killers. They just chalk him up as another statistic."

Amelia nodded. She knew exactly what Viola Richards was talking about. Young black men, drug dealer or no drug dealer, were all statistics. They would lump their deaths in one of two categories: drug related or gang related.

"I take it that you don't have great faith in our police department," Amelia observed.

"Could as well been them that killed my baby," Viola told her.

Amelia nodded. Good. She now knew that Viola was no fan of the police department, which meant that in all probability she would cooperate with her request.

"Any idea who did this to your son?"

Viola shook her head. "No, it could have been anybody. You know how things are; nobody wants to be a snitch. It could be your best friend, your mama, even your own child. That's just the way it is."

"Take care of it in the streets, huh?"

Mrs. Richards nodded. "But the only problem with that is that it's just more kids getting killed."

Amelia nodded. "I believe in taking care of our own."

Amelia led Viola to the upper level of the parking garage and stopped just in front of a black Mercedes S Class. "Are you a religious woman, Mrs. Richards?"

"Of course. I go to church every Sunday."

"Sometimes God has a plan for each of us. And sometimes we don't understand what His plan is. Sometimes he works in ways so mysterious, even we doctors can't explain it."

"Amen! I know that's right."

"Sometimes when we doctors have exhausted all medical means possible, God steps in with His hand and touches a person.

Even when we have given up, sometimes God says *I ain't done using this person yet.*"

Viola smiled. "I know that my Quadir is with the Lord. I know that God still has a plan for him, and for each of us." She clasped Amelia's hand and shook it. "I want to thank you for all that you did to try to save my son."

Amelia smiled. "Don't thank me just yet. You may want to lean up against this car right here."

Viola leaned back against the Mercedes and stared at Amelia. She was truly puzzled.

"After the surgeon worked on your son, he thought that he had lost him. He declared your son deceased. A short time later, an orderly went into the room and found that your son was not dead."

Viola clasped her chest and her knees buckled. Amelia caught her and held her up.

"I rushed into the operating room, and I began to operate on your son. I found the bullet that the surgeon could not retrieve, and I was able to repair the damage to your son."

Viola stared at her in bewilderment.

Amelia smiled and nodded. "Quadir is alive," she whispered.

Viola gasped and began to slide to the ground again. Amelia could not hold her up this time. Tears flowed from Viola's eyes, and she began to kiss Amelia's hands. "Thank you, thank you, thank you! Oh, dear Lord, thank you! My baby is alive! Thank you!"

Amelia knelt down beside her. "We don't know who tried to kill Quadir. We have to be very, very careful. I want to keep him alive. I don't want to tell anyone that he is alive, understand?"

Viola nodded.

"I don't know who I can trust. Does he have a wife?"

Viola frowned at the thought of Gena. She never had liked the girl, but that was her son's choice, not hers. "He has a girlfriend and they were engaged, but they hadn't tied the knot. Even still, though, I don't want to tell nobody! Nobody! Don't call nobody else, doc."

Amelia nodded. "I haven't informed the police."

"Good! Don't tell them neither!"

"Quadir is in stable but critical condition. These next few days are going to be really important for him."

"Can I see him, doctor?"

"Eventually, yes. But right now, to have you coming up to the hospital . . ."

She nodded again. "I understand. Just do whatever it is you're doing. Just keep doing your thing, baby!" Viola wrapped her arms around Amelia and hugged her as tight as she could.

"I love you," Viola began crying heavily. "I don't know you, but I love you, baby. I love you so much. You brought my baby back to me."

Amelia rose and helped Viola to her feet. "We are going to have to be smart on this one."

"Whatever you need, baby, you just tell me."

"We can't let anyone catch on, especially the fiancée. We can't let her snoop around. I've taken care of the autopsy report. The death certificate has already been signed by another doctor. I have a body from the morgue with Quadir's chart on it."

"A body."

"He was a John Doe. No one has claimed him for some time. He was young, about Quadir's age, decent shape. Probably homeless, maybe even a drug addict. He probably has no family, so to speak, and his looks are perfect to allow him to pass for Quadir."

Mrs. Richardson nodded solemnly.

"So, tomorrow you can have the undertaker pick him up, okay," Amelia asked, hoping Quadir's mother was following her line. "And you'll take care of the fiancée, right? Make sure she doesn't make trouble for us."

"Oh, I think I can handle that. I can definitely keep her from getting into things. Once I get into his house, I can control everything." *The first thing will be to put her ass out. Once I get rid of Gena, everything will work itself out,* Viola couldn't help but think to herself. "Mmm-hmm, I can get in there, control things. Keep her from his papers, his money, and all the things that she can use to mess things up for us."

Amelia nodded.

Viola bounced up and down slightly. "I can't believe my baby is alive!"

Amelia nodded.

"When can I see him?"

"I'll call you and let you know. Once he's fully conscious, and feeling a lot better, I'll get you into the hospital."

"Was there any permanent damage to anything? I mean, don't get me wrong. I'll take him as a vegetable, as long as he's alive."

"I understand. It's a perfectly normal question. Right now, I think that only time will tell. I don't believe that there will be any permanent damage, but again, time will let us know. He will need therapy, lots of rehabilitation, a good diet of soft foods at first."

"Are you going to see it through?"

"Huh?"

"I know how things go. You're a doctor; you have other patients. I just don't want you to pass him on down the line to a bunch of other doctors and therapists and who knows who else. I want you to look after my baby."

Amelia nodded. "I'll see him through, Mrs. Richards. I'll see him through."

Viola hugged Amelia once again. "What church do you go to?"

"I go to First Baptist in Germantown," Amelia replied.

"Come to church with me this Sunday. Please."

Amelia hesitated for several moments, and then relented. "Okay, I'll go."

"Thank you, so much." Viola kissed the doctor on her cheek. "Your parents must be so proud of you! I'm so proud of you, and I just met you! Where are you from?"

"Alabama."

"Alabama! Wow, you sure are far away from home. Do you have any family in these parts?"

Amelia shook her head. "No, just my patients."

"You poor, sweet thing, I want you to come to dinner at our house on Sunday after church! You can just call your folks in Alabama and tell them that you got stolen by a crazy lady in Philadelphia! I'm adopting your butt! I know you like soul food!"

Amelia nodded. "Raised on it."

"Girl, my collard greens will make you wanna slap your mama!"

Amelia threw her head back and laughed. She liked Viola. She knew then and there that she had just found a foster family in her new city.

DR. DO GOOD

Amelia rushed into Quadir's hospital room, closing the door behind her.

"Your name is John Smith. Do you understand me?"

"What?"

"I said your name is John Smith."

"Why do you keep telling me that?" Quadir asked.

"I'm telling you again today, in case you didn't understand me the other day. You were still a little out of it. But understand me, this is extremely important."

"Why?"

"Because someone tried to kill you, and because I sent Quadir Richards's body to a funeral home, where they held a funeral service for it and buried it almost two weeks ago. Quadir Richards is dead. John Smith, someone whom no one wants dead, is alive and well in the hospital. Understand?"

Quadir nodded. "Why?"

"Why what?"

"Why are you trying to help me?"

"Let's just say I promised someone that I would see things through."

There was a knock at the door.

"Come in," Amelia shouted.

The door opened, and two gentlemen in white hospital coats walked in.

"How's he doing today?" one of them asked.

Amelia nodded. "Cranky. But alive."

"That's a good sign." He extended his hand to Quadir. "Hello, young man. My name is Dr. Benjamin Brant. How are you feeling today?"

Quadir nodded. "Doing pretty well, doc."

"Well, that's good to hear. Any pain anywhere?"

"No."

"That's good. You feel any discomfort, you let the nurses know, and they'll give you something for the pain. We want you to be as comfortable as possible."

"Thank you, doc."

"Don't thank me; thank Dr. Hopkins over there. She's the one who saved your life. You're a very lucky young man, you know that? You're fortunate that she was here that day."

Quadir turned and stared at her. She was young, black, and country as all out backwoods. He had thought that she was a nurse or something. But the doctor was now telling him that she was a doctor, too. A surgeon, in fact the surgeon who saved his life. *Ain't this a bitch?*

Amelia lifted Quadir's chart. "I want you to go easy on the medication. I've written up the orders to start your therapy today."

Amelia turned and waved her hand toward the second gentleman in the room. "This is Neal Ryan, your physical therapist. Neal is the best we have here at Hahnemann Hospital, and probably the best in Philly. He's going to get you back up and running in no time."

Neal extended his hand to Quadir. "Pleasure to meet you, Mr. Smith."

Quadir clasped Neal's hand and shook it.

"We're going to have you back up to a hundred percent before you know it," Neal told him. "Can you move your leg for me?"

"Well, I'll leave you guys alone. I have some more patients to peek in on," Dr. Brant told them. He patted Quadir's arm. "You get better, young man. I'll see you tomorrow."

"Thank you, doc," Quadir said.

Brant exited the room, leaving Quadir, Neal, and Amelia alone.

"Okay, try to move your leg again for me," Neal said.

Quadir stared down at his legs, but neither of them moved. "I can't move them, I can't move my legs!"

"Relax, it just takes time." Neal reassured him.

"Relax? What the fuck do you mean, relax? I can't move my fucking legs!"

"Okay, calm down," Neal told him.

"I can't move my legs!" Quadir cried out.

Neal turned toward Amelia.

"He's not paralyzed." Amelia shook her head. "There may be some internal scarring that we didn't know about. I'll order some X-rays."

Neal placed his hand beneath Quadir's leg and bent it. "I can feel your nerves jumping and your muscles contracting. Try to force your leg straight."

Quadir's face contorted as he tried to force his leg straight.

Neal turned to Amelia and shook his head. Nothing.

Amelia examined Quadir's chart. She made several nota-
tions on it. "I'm modifying your diet. Right now I have you
on liquids and soft foods. I'm going to slowly adjust it to in-
clude more and more solids. I want to increase your proteins
and lean foods. Also, I'm ordering a dietary supplement to be
given twice a day."

"I'm going to add the pool to his therapy regimen also,"
Neal told her. "I think starting him off slow with some water
resistance would be good." He faced Quadir. "From what I
can tell, your muscles have been used to doing nothing for the
past few weeks. We're just going to have to whip them back
into shape. I want to get you down there into our therapeutic
pool and get you started today. It's a heated pool, really warm
water, and it should feel good to your body. It may also cause
the internal swelling to go down a bit. How's that sound?"

"Like a bunch of medical bullshit!" Quadir told him.

Neal smiled. "I'm going to run and get the pool ready, take
care of some paperwork, and I'll be back with a wheelchair."

Neal turned and exited the room. Amelia replaced Quadir's
chart.

"I'm paralyzed," Quadir said flatly, unable to believe it, and
at that very moment wishing he was dead.

"You are not."

"Bullshit! I can't move my legs!"

"I'm the doctor here, and I'm telling you that you're not
paralyzed! You're just lazy."

"Oh, like I wanna be stuck in this fucking bed!"

"Why is it that when Dr. Brant or one of the white doctors
come around, it's yes, sir, no, sir, thank you, doctor. But with

me, it's fuck, bullshit, and every other curse word that you can think of?"

"What?"

"Is it because I'm young, black, or a woman? What is it? Whatever happened to manners?"

"No, it's because I can't move my legs and I'd rather be dead than paralyzed."

Amelia couldn't help but smile. He was an asshole. "You're a bitch, you know that?"

"I'm a bitch? I didn't know doctors called their patients bitches now days."

"This one calls them like she sees them. You're more than just a bitch; you're a punk bitch. You bow down and suck up to the white man, but you treat me like shit."

"What?"

"You're one of them house niggas, aren't you. You'll pick up a gun, and you'll aim it at another black man, but you'll throw that bitch down and put ya hands up when the white man comes around."

"Fuck you! You don't know me! You don't know shit about me, or who I am!"

Amelia nodded. "I know you. I know your type. Big bad brave man, tough with a gun. Quick with ya mouth. But when it really comes down to it, you ain't shit. You ain't a real built-to-last nigga. You're a quitter and a coward."

Quadir tried to sit up. "Bitch, you don't know me! I ain't nobody's fucking coward!"

"Coward!"

Quadir sat up, clasped the bed rail, took his free hand, and swung his legs off the side of the bed.

"You want to know something, Quadir?"

"What?" Quadir snapped.

"A paralyzed man wouldn't be able to sit up in bed."

Quadir looked down and examined himself. He caught on to what she had done.

"You're not a coward. You're a fighter. The way you were going to come after me, that's the same determination that you have to use to regain all your abilities. You have to fight for your life again. Fight to get it back! If you are counting on some medicine or some magic potion or formula to give it back to you, it ain't going to happen. Sorry, brother, but nothing like that has been invented yet. You're going to have to fight."

"You should be a motivational speaker," he said sarcastically.

"You should sell shit to mushroom farms, 'cause you're really an asshole."

Quadir laughed. She was sharp. He had tried her. Tried to push her buttons, disrespected her, doubted her even. But it was now obvious that she was the real deal.

"Do you want to walk again?" Amelia asked.

Quadir shrugged his shoulders. "I don't know."

She had heard that answer before. She had done volunteer work the previous summer in Chad. Many soldiers had given her the same answer. Walk again for what? To go back out there and face a world that would still be just as hard, just as hostile to them? She knew where his answer was coming from.

"You don't know, because what would change, huh? What would be different in the world if you went back out there again? Everything would be just the same, all of the bullshit would be exactly the same. Am I right?"

Quadir shifted his gaze toward her.

"One thing would be different. You. You would know that

you took what the world threw at you, and you handled it. You get up, go back out there, and you smile at that fucked-up world, and you let it know that it didn't defeat you. Let them know that they may have knocked you down, but that you got right back up. Let them know that you are a real soldier, a warrior for your people! You may encounter defeats, but you must not be defeated!"

"You're quoting Maya Angelou now."

Amelia recoiled slightly. She had been taken by surprise. "How did you know that?"

"I can read."

"I'm shocked."

"That I can read?"

"That you would know Maya. Most guys your age . . ."

"I guess we both made the mistake of prejudging each other."

"I guess we did."

Neal walked into the room pushing a wheelchair. "Wow, look at you sitting up!" He parked the chair next to Quadir's bed and then helped him into it. "Be back in a while, doc."

Amelia nodded.

Quadir stopped the chair just before they were about to exit and turned back toward her.

"No more prejudging each other?"

"No more prejudging each other."

Neal looked at them strangely.

Quadir smiled and shook his head. "You're a pain in the ass, doc. And that's no prejudgment."

Amelia threw her head back and laughed. "And you are an asshole, Mr. Smith. A bona fide asshole who's full of shit."

Quadir wheeled himself out of the room smiling.

THE GOOD FOOT

Amelia strolled into the physical therapy room and spied Quadir in a nearby corner with Neal. Neal had Quadir lying on his back on a mat, while Neal was pushing his leg forward, shouting for Quadir to push. He had been in therapy for only a few days now, and results had been slow in coming. Quadir was not physically disabled. He was simply indifferent to trying. He acted as though he simply wanted to give up.

She approached and stood over him. "Lying on your ass again, huh?"

"Now is not the time for humor," Quadir told her.

"Any time is a good time for humor. How's he coming along, Neal?"

"If he would put as much effort into his therapy as he did into resisting it, he'd be ready to run a marathon right now."

Amelia nodded. "So, what's the deal, Quadir?"

"Ain't no deal."

"Push," Neal ordered.

"I am pushing; can't you tell?"

"You're not pushing. I know that you got more in you than this. Hey, if you don't want to walk, that's your problem. I can't make you walk."

"Then why don't you just leave me alone. I was fine lying in my bed watching TV. You came and got me, remember?"

"A regular wiseass," Neal said, peering up at Amelia.

"I already know."

"Aren't you like a surgeon or something?" Quadir asked. "Shouldn't you be somewhere cutting somebody open, and charging them an arm and a leg for it?"

"Neal, let me take over for a little while," Amelia told him.

Neal nodded. He was happy to be rid of Quadir Richards, if only for today. "Be my guest, please!"

"Hang close, I'm going to need you to help me get him into his chair."

"I'll be right across the room if you need me," said Neal.

Amelia turned to Quadir. "I thought that we had this conversation already."

"And what conversation is that?"

"The conversation about you being a quitter."

"We didn't converse. You talked; I listened."

"Funny. So are you going to be a coward and just give up?"

"I thought you said that I wasn't a coward?"

"All quitters are cowards."

"Kenny Rogers said that you got to know when to fold 'em."

"So, your life is a game of cards now?"

"Life has always been nothing but one big gamble."

"So you fold, huh? Gonna go back to your room, cash in all of your chips, and call it quits? I wish I would have known you were a quitter before. I wouldn't have wasted my time."

"Why did you?"

"Because I saw a man who wouldn't quit! Because I saw a man who refused to give up, a man who refused to die! I thought you were a fighter."

"It's real easy to stand there and judge somebody! You haven't been through what I've been through!"

"Oh, you poor baby! You got shot. So the fuck what! So now what are you going to do? Are you going to get back on the goddamned bike, or what?"

"What?"

"You heard me! What are you going to do, Quadir? When little kids get a boo boo, they get up, dust themselves off, get back out there, and keep going. What are you going to do, little boy? 'Cause frankly, just about everybody in here is tired of your whiney attitude. It's time to either shit or get off the pot!"

Quadir went for his wheelchair. He pulled it close, put the brakes on it, and then pulled himself up onto it. The therapists in the room clapped when he was finished. Quadir looked at Amelia as if he wanted to kill her.

"I don't need your fucking help! Yours and nobody else's!"

"You owe these people in here more than that! You owe them more than your scorn. You owe a whole lot of people some goddamned effort!"

"Everyone keeps telling me what I owe. Everyone keeps telling me how grateful I should be, how good of a goddamned doctor you are, but you know what? I can't see it! All I see is a fucking pain in the ass!"

"You fucking quitter. If you don't believe that you owe these people who have spent all of their time taking care of you, trying to get you better, then maybe I can take you to somebody who you do think you owe something to!"

Amelia grabbed Quadir's chair, turned him around, and pushed him out the room. She headed down the hall, out of the therapy ward, around a few corners, and into the chapel.

"What do you think you're doing?" Quadir asked.

"When's the last time you sat and prayed, Quadir?"

"I prayed the other night."

"You should pray every day."

"Don't tell me what I need to do. What are you, a priest *and* a doctor?"

"If I were a priest, I would drown your ass in some holy water."

Quadir smiled.

"Someone wants to see you. Since you don't feel like you owe any of us any effort, then maybe you'll try to get better for her." Amelia pushed him all the way into the chapel.

A woman rose from her knees, turned, and smiled at him.

"Mom!" Quadir's eyes flew open wide with amazement and surprise.

Viola's tears flowed, as she rushed to him.

"Baby!" She leaned forward and embraced her son tightly. "You really are alive. Thank you, Lord! Thank you!"

She pulled Amelia close and hugged her. "Thank you so much! Thank you for saving my baby!"

"Now we just have to get your baby to want to save himself," Amelia told her.

"What do you mean?" Viola asked.

"Tell her, Quadir."

"Tell me what?" Viola said as she shifted back and forth between the two of them. "What's going on, Quadir?"

Quadir smacked his lips. "Nothing; she's just crazy, that's all."

"Quadir, Amelia has been over to my house many times since we've met."

"What?" Quadir recoiled.

Amelia smiled at him.

"And she may be many things, but one thing she is not is crazy. What is going on?"

"Do you want to tell her, or should I?" Amelia asked looking at Quadir.

"Do what you want; you've been doing it anyhow."

Viola could see her son's attitude and placed her hand on her hip as she looked down on him.

"Quadir here has given up." Amelia told her.

"What?"

"Yep, he's thrown in the towel. Doesn't want to try in therapy, just wants to sit back and eat Jell-O and watch television."

"No, that's not my son. My son is a not a quitter. My baby's a fighter!"

The two women stared at Quadir in silence. He could feel their eyes on him.

"Quadir . . ." Viola started off.

"Okay, okay!"

"Okay what?" Amelia asked. "You admit to your mother that you're a quitter, or okay, you're not going to let her down and be a quitter."

Quadir peered up at her and rolled his eyes at Amelia. She was the most nerve-racking woman he had ever met.

"Baby, I want you to walk out of this hospital on your own two feet," Viola told him. "I want you to hurry up and get well and get outta this place."

Quadir nodded.

"His gunshot wounds are healing rather well," Amelia explained. "He has one that I left open, because of infection. We pack it twice a day, and we've been giving him antibiotics for it. I want it to close up on its own. It'll leave only a slightly larger scar than if we had sewn it up. But he's coming along rather nicely."

Viola caressed Quadir's head and nodded.

"We just need for him to give us some effort, so we can get him walking."

"I'm sore and it hurts like hell!" Quadir told her.

"Just try, baby. Do it for me. Just promise me that you'll try," Viola pleaded.

Quadir nodded. "Okay, I'll do it."

"Good." Amelia smiled. "Well, I'll leave you two alone so that you can catch up. I'll be back in, say . . . thirty minutes?"

"Thank you so much, Amelia," Mrs. Richards leaned forward and kissed her on her cheek.

Amelia turned and left the chapel.

"How's Gena doing?" Quadir asked.

"She's doing good. She's just fine."

"Where is she? Why didn't she come here with you?"

"Baby, after this happened to you, I didn't trust nobody. I decided it be best and I let her think you were dead."

"What? That's Gena! Why would you do that?"

"Baby, I know. But it was for your own safety."

"My safety? She didn't shoot me!"

"Listen, I didn't even tell your father and no I didn't tell her. Do you know what could happen if Gena finds out you're alive? Do you understand that Amelia put her entire medical career on the line to help protect you? If Gena knew you were alive, the entire city would know. There's no way she could keep this kind of secret. Please trust us, trust me, and trust Dr. Hopkins. Don't worry about Gena. You just go ahead and get well. I want you to walk out of this place, then go get your precious Gena and get the hell outta Philly."

"Get outta Philly? Where's Rik? Where's Rasun?"

"Baby, you can worry about them after you get better! But, son, you got to understand, you're a ghost to these people. To them, you don't exist."

Quadir nodded. "I want to see Gena."

"I know you do. I know, son, but she's fine; she's tough, and she can handle herself until you get yourself together and figure out where to go from here with your life."

Quadir thought about his money. He knew he had been out of it for weeks. He knew that rent needed to be paid, mortgages needed to be paid, and all his other bills had to be taken care of.

"I need you to take care of a few things for me."

"What?"

"I need you to pay some bills for me."

"I already took care of all that, Quadir."

"All of them?"

Viola nodded. She thought that she had in fact taken care of all her son's bills, not knowing he had many others she knew nothing about, one important one in particular.

"Quadir, I've taken care of everything. You just relax, do your therapy, son, and get better. Okay, baby?"

Quadir nodded. He would do as she said. He would focus and he would hurry up and get the hell out of that hospital. Either that or he was going to catch a case for killing Dr. Hopkins.

Viola maneuvered herself behind her son's wheelchair and began to push. "I want you to come up to the front of the chapel with me so we can pray together, okay?"

Quadir looked blankly at his mother. He didn't know what she expected of him, but he didn't have any prayers left. He had prayed, prayed more than anyone would ever know. Every time he tried to use his legs to hold him up, he prayed. And every time he tried to take a step, he prayed. *Don't she know all I been doing is praying?* He knew his mother and he also knew that even if he didn't want to, Viola wouldn't take no for an answer.

"Okay."

CAN'T GET RIGHT

Six Weeks Later

Dr. Hopkins strolled into her patient's room pushing a wheelchair.

"Up and at 'em, sleepyhead."

Quadir was lying on his bed, staring out the window. He turned to face her.

"You are a pest. You should get an award for being the peskiest doctor in the world. Why you won't stop?"

"Because, Mr. Smith, you are a fighter. You fought for your life on that operating table, and now it's time to fight for getting back into the game of life. So, up, up, up."

Amelia lowered the bed railing and clasped Quadir's arm. He snatched it away from her.

"You're not even my doctor anymore. And you're not my therapist. I don't feel like it today!"

"Look, Mr. Smith, I didn't save your ass to see you sit here and wither away. Now stop acting like a little bitch and get your fucking ass in the wheelchair."

Quadir frowned at her, trying to figure out why she was constantly calling him Mr. Smith. *Damn, she won't stop; she just won't stop.*

"You're like the Energizer bunny. You should wear a bunny outfit and get some Rollerblades," he said, laughing at her. "Look, you could roll down the hall and shit, in and out of all your patients' rooms, constantly being a disturbance, you know how you do," he said, looking at her with his eyebrows raised, waiting for her to agree with his jokes.

"You know what? You really are an asshole."

"And you're really a pain in my ass. You know what, doc, that's all the fuck I do feel, the pain in my ass from your constant bullshit."

"Get the fuck up, and get in the goddamn chair," she hollered as she took his vitals chart and used it as a weapon, ready to attack him.

"Please, you can't hit me; you're a doctor and I'm a sick patient."

"Get your ass up and get in the chair! I'm not leaving until we're done."

"Fuck, man, come on," he said huffing and puffing, but he did it because he knew she had to win and she wouldn't stop. She meant every word she said. He sulked his way off the bed and into the wheelchair.

She pushed him to the elevator and they made the short trip to the rehabilitation center.

"Can I just pay you for your services?" Quadir asked.

"Are you serious?" She stopped the chair and walked around in front of him. "You could never repay me. Do you understand that, Mr. Smith?" she said, looking like Bette Davis.

"Yo, you ever see that movie *What Ever Happened to Baby Jane?* That's you." He started laughing at her again.

This black man must be out of his mind.

"I got your Baby Jane; shut up before I really show you how Bette I can get," she said, slapping the back of his head.

"I'm going file a report against you. That's the second time you've hit me."

"Listen, Mr. Smith, I'm really tired of your shit. I know you can do this. I know you can. If you could come back and cheat death the way you did, I know you can make a full recovery. I know you can. Gosh, if you believed in yourself as much as I do, you'd have walked out of here by now. Now come on, it's showtime."

She hit a button on the wall and the double doors to the rehab center in the west wing of the hospital opened. She wheeled him up to a set of walking bars.

"Okay, here we go. God, do you believe all that energy? You are so draining, Mr. Smith, I mean really," she said as she unbuckled him, raised the foot bars, and gently set his feet on the floor.

She set the brakes on the wheelchair, unbuckled Quadir, and pulled him out of the chair. Quadir gripped the bars tightly, holding on for dear life. Amelia made her way behind him, and placed her hands on his waist.

"How many times are you going to bring me down here to do this?" Quadir said, gritting his teeth. "I can't do it yet!"

"You can do anything you put your mind to. You can do this, Quadir. You're stronger than you even know. I watched a soldier who refused to give in, who stared death in the face and told it to go to hell. You can do this. One step, Quadir, it just takes one step."

Quadir closed his eyes and gritted his teeth again. He wanted this pesky, silly bitch gone and out of his life. He wanted to be alone and if he had to be around someone, he wanted it to be someone who would understand what he was going through. He wanted Gena.

"Don't look at me like that. Only a coward gives up, Quadir."

A coward? Is she calling me a fucking coward?

"What? You heard me; you're not even trying. A fucking coward, I can't believe this shit," she huffed under her breath, loud enough for him to hear.

Bitch, please. He couldn't help it. She must be crazy to offer such an analysis. Quadir had been through more than Amelia Hopkins could ever dream about. He was a soldier, a warrior, and a gangster to the fullest. He ate niggas for breakfast, and bitches like her were nothing but a midmorning snack.

"You going to let a bar beat you?" Amelia asked.

"Shut up!" Quadir exploded. "Will you just shut the fuck up!"

"That's right! Get angry! But what are you going to do with all that anger? Are you going to yell at me and sit back down and quit? Or are you going to get angry at the people who tried to take life away from you, the people who put you in this wheelchair? Are you going to let them win? Are you going to let them beat you, Quadir?"

Quadir breathed in heavily and gripped the bars tightly. He lifted himself up as much as he could, while staring at his right foot.

Move, dammit, move, he commanded.

And it did.

The left foot slowly followed, and then the right one. He

walked to the end of the track and turned around gasping for air. He was exhausted.

"Oh, my God. No, no, stay there. Oh, my God. Quadir, oh, my God. That's good for one day; just stay right there. I'll bring the chair to you," said Amelia in amazement and disbelief.

"No, leave the chair where it's at," Quadir told her. He stared at his feet again and willed them to move.

Amelia cupped her hands over her mouth, as tears begin to stream down her face. These were the moments she lived and breathed for. These were the moments that made every sacrifice in her life worthwhile. She watched as Quadir took four tiny steps and collapsed into her arms.

"Yes! Yes! I knew that you could do it!" She hugged him as if he were her child, taking his first baby steps in life.

Quadir held on to her, hugging her back and fighting back his own tears. He wanted to cry, he wanted to cry so bad, but Baby Jane wouldn't have that on him. He had shown her; he had walked. He couldn't believe he had walked. He hugged Amelia tightly, kissing her cheek, and he felt her kiss his cheek back. And out of all the hugging and kissing, their lips met, and she kissed him back, a long and passionate kiss. Amelia completely forgot her position and role as a doctor; she didn't even realize the road that they had started down in that one kiss.

The next day, after her rounds, Amelia entered Quadir's room with her trusty wheelchair and was met with a happy face.

"I take it you're ready."

"Might as well be; I don't have no choice."

"Well, today, I have a surprise for you," she said, helping

him into the chair, as she placed his feet on the foot holders. She pushed him down the hall and onto the elevator as usual, but this time when the doors opened she made a left instead of a right.

"Where we going?"

"I told you I had a surprise for you today."

Amelia took her patient for a stroll through the hospital's gardens, hoping that some fresh air would do him good. He had accomplished so much in such a short period of time. His recovery bordered on miraculous.

She stopped his wheelchair next to a bench in front of a statue commemorating the hospital's founder. She took a seat on the bench close to him.

"Are we about to have *the* conversation?" Quadir asked.

"And which conversation is that? We have a couple of them that we need to have."

Quadir laughed. "I guess you're right. But I figured you were strolling me out here so that we could talk about why I'm here and why someone would try to kill me. You know, that conversation."

"Those things have crossed my mind a few times."

"Well, you know my name, and I'm pretty sure you know my date of birth." Quadir peered off into the distance. "It's pretty hard to know where to start. I mean, you already know all my personal information. Not to mention, you operated on me; you saved my life."

Amelia nodded and laughed. "Yeah, I guess I know a few things. I'll admit that."

Quadir shrugged. "I don't know. I really don't know where to start."

"Would you rather I ask you?"

"I don't know. I guess that probably would be better."

"Do you have a nickname?"

"Yeah, sort of, Qua, sometimes Q."

"Is that what all of your friends called you? Qua?"

Quadir nodded.

"Are you originally from Philly?"

"Yeah, I was born at Pennsylvania Hospital downtown. I grew up in North Philly my entire life. Where are you from?"

Amelia exhaled and peered off into the distance.

"I'm a country girl, straight off the farm in Alabama."

"How did you wind up in Philly?"

"I wanted more, I guess. I just couldn't see myself working on my parents' farm for the rest of my life, or marrying some drugstore clerk in the nearest town and cranking out babies for the next twenty years of my life. Not much out there in the country. So, after high school I got accepted to Temple University and then took up my residence at Temple University Hospital. After completing my residency, I got offered a job here at Hahnemann, so I decided to stay in Philadelphia and see how things worked out. I've been here at Hahnemann now for five years."

"That's good; that's really good. You stayed focused. Sometimes, I wish I had stuck it out and stayed in school."

"Why, you dropped out of high school?" Amelia questioned.

"No, I graduated with honors from high school. And I went on to college at the University of Delaware."

"Did you graduate?"

"Yeah."

"Really?" asked Amelia. She had never thought for one second that Quadir had a formal education.

"I got my bachelor's and after that I wanted to go to grad school to become a dentist. But, I guess I got sidetracked."

"What do you mean by that?"

"Well, I struggled to get through school. It wasn't like I came from money. My pops hustled in the streets. He did the number game and had speakeasies in the city, and while we wasn't poor, we wasn't rich neither. I guess after I graduated and I came back home to Philly, I saw everybody hustling, getting fast money, you know, and I wanted a piece of it. I always said I'd go back to school and become a dentist and open my own office someday. I just got sidetracked and one thing led to another."

"I see it led you right here to my operating table."

"Yeah, I always thought I was invincible. I never saw myself shot up and in a wheelchair. I have a friend, Christopher Cole, who we all called Forty, and he was kidnapped last year and held for a million-dollar ransom. Even though I paid his ransom, his kidnappers still shot him up and left him for dead. I remember going to visit him in the hospital. His body looked weak and frail and he was all beat up and bandaged up and the doctors said he'd never walk again, and to this day, he's still in a wheelchair. But I'll never forget the day I went to see him after he had been shot up and I knew then that I didn't want this life. I knew then that I didn't want to end up like that."

"So what did you do?"

"I stopped. I gave up the life, and I stopped selling drugs."

"Really?"

"Yeah, and you know what's so ironic, I ended up shot and in a wheelchair anyway."

"Well, you know we're gonna work on that, right?"

"Hey, I'm surprised you let me outside."

Amelia couldn't help but laugh. "Yeah, you're lucky, real lucky."

"In more ways than you could ever know."

"I just don't understand why you would choose to sell drugs. Of all the things you could do to make your life better, you chose that."

"Don't do that."

"Don't do what?"

"Don't judge me. I hate that. People always think of drug dealers being these low-life scum buckets, and that, for the most part is never the case."

"I'm not attempting to judge you, Quadir. I'm just trying to understand."

"That's just it. It's something that you can never understand. The life I live, and the life these brothers is out here living in these streets, can't be explained or understood. Not from sitting on a park bench on a nice side of town, beneath an oak tree."

"I guess I deserved that. I guess I can never understand the world that you come from, but I can learn more about it."

"Why would you want to?"

"Why do you live it? All bullshit aside, you're smarter than that. You're a very intelligent man who could do so many things with his life. Really, that's what I don't get. You're smart, you're fearless, you're young and handsome. The world would lie down for you, if you asked it to. Why not go out and do bigger things?"

Quadir leaned back in his chair. He was at a loss for words. He didn't know how to feel about Amelia. She was drop-dead gorgeous, a dime to say the least. And she was a hell of a surgeon. The fact that he was still breathing testified to that. She was smart, and dedicated, and she was straight up. She didn't act all high and mighty, like some bourgeois bitches, after they had finished college. And what was really tripping him out was that she really seemed to care about him. Not just about getting him back up and walking again, but about his life and his future. She was challenging him physically, mentally, and emotionally. He had never had a woman do that before.

"C'mon, let's get you back inside before those bitches in the recovery ward start tripping."

Quadir threw his head back in laughter. "I have never heard a doctor like you before."

"I'm the new generation of doctors. We kick ass. We heal it, but we kick it too." Amelia rose from the bench and began to push Quadir back into the hospital. "Don't make me have to fuck you up behind your therapy, either. 'Cause you know I will."

"And you said you're the new generation, huh?"

"And don't get it twisted."

FULLY LOADED

Amelia tossed Quadir a towel so that he could wipe the sweat from his brow. He quickened his pace on the treadmill to a rapid jog.

"Okay, Jesse Owens, let's not overdo it," she told him.

"Relax, doc. I'm one hundred percent. Plus, I had a pretty good therapist who whipped me back into shape."

Amelia tilted her head and smiled. "Good try, but flattery will get you nowhere." She climbed onto a nearby stair stepper and began exercising. "I'm going to check and make sure your wounds are healing okay. I don't want them to reopen from the inside—that could just be the worst."

"Will you stop worrying? Doc, you did your thing. The Q is back!"

"All right, Qua. Let's just hope that he's here to stay. It'd be a shame to have to take you back to the hospital because your gigantic ego burst open your stitches."

Quadir joined in the laughter. He flipped the off switch on

the treadmill and walked to the stair stepper, where he lifted the doc into the air.

"Boy, what are you doing?" she shouted. "You can't lift me, I'm too heavy. You'll rip your insides for sure."

"Heavy? What do you weigh, a buck fifteen at the most? And that's probably with all your clothes on and soaking wet." Quadir set her down.

"Watch your wounds, please," Amelia said in all seriousness as she turned to face him.

"Why? I got the best doctor in the land."

"I know that's right. See, I knew you was a smart man."

"What made you want to become a doctor?" Quadir asked.

"It was all I could think of being when I was a little girl. My first little plastic stethoscope had me hooked."

"Man, that's a lot of schooling, though. How'd you stay focused?"

"I don't know; I just did," Amelia said.

"I know your family is proud."

"Oh, God, yes. You should see my father. He has an entire photo collection of me in his wallet. He's really my biggest fan."

Quadir sat down on a weight bench, grabbed the towel again, and wiped the sweat from his brow.

"This is a really nice gym you got here."

"Thanks, I figured since I don't have any children, no roommates, and no pets, I'd turn the spare room into my own fitness center. Why pay for a gym, you know?"

Quadir looked at Amelia as she lay on her back counting crunches as she moved her upper body off the floor and then back down again. She really was quite amazing. She was

not only beautiful, but also smart, practical, financially independent, and full of determination. After Quadir's extended
stay in the inpatient rehabilitation center of Hahnemann, he
was upgraded to outpatient status. It was then that Amelia
brought him home with her, where she and her housekeeper
could nurse him back to health.

"Doctors must make a lot of money."

"We do pretty good. I think the industry is suffering, you
know, with insurance and HMOs and all that, but yeah, we
make an honest living."

"Well, if this is an honest living, I've been wasting my time
in them streets."

"Why you say that?"

"Yo, this is a mansion. Your house is absolutely amazing.
You sure you just a doctor?"

"Of course; don't be silly."

"Damn, I'm in the wrong profession. If motherfuckers in
the hood could see this shit here, they'd all be signing up for
medical school."

"Really."

"Really," Quadir responded, looking around the weight
room.

Outside the door from where he sat was a sauna, a steam
room, and an indoor swimming pool that had a retractable
glass top, making it an outdoor swimming pool on warm,
sunny summer days.

"Why me, though?"

"What do you mean, why you?"

"What I said. Everything you've done for me, saving my
life, fighting to make me walk again, against my own will, and
bringing me to your home. You didn't have to do half of the

stuff that you've done for me. So, I'm just a little curious as to why you're helping me."

Amelia looked Quadir in the eyes and realized she didn't really have the answer.

"I don't know. I guess maybe because you needed someone to help you. I just wanted to help, that's all," she said as she gently caressed the side of his face. "Is that okay with you?"

"Yeah, it's just that where I come from most people ain't into putting themselves out there to help anyone. Help is the last thing you're gonna get."

"Well, for me, being a doctor, I guess it's in my blood."

"Thank you; thank you for everything."

"You don't have to say that, but you're welcome."

They both sat in silence as Amelia wrapped up her crunches and Quadir thought about his life. All that he had done and all that he had been through could make a best-selling novel. *I should write a book.*

Amelia finished her last crunch, hopped up from the floor, and stood towering over Quadir.

"Hey, I got to hurry up and get to the hospital, make my rounds, and check out for the day. Is there anything you'd like me to get you while I'm out?"

"No, no, I'm fine. But I do have a favor to ask of you."

"Sure, what is it?" she said, facing him with all seriousness.

"I was wondering if I could borrow your car."

"Ready to rock and roll, huh?"

"No, no, not like that, just get out, you know, move around a little."

"I understand, but Quadir, you do understand that you cannot afford for anyone to see you. You're Mr. Smith and until you have some minor plastic surgery, you really need to stay inside and out of sight."

"I'll stay low; trust me."

Amelia stared straight through him as her mind wandered off.

"Well, I guess it's okay. But, take my black BMW. It has tinted windows, so that way I don't have to worry about you being spotted. Geez, Quadir, don't you know the chances you're taking?"

"Listen, I got this. Trust me. I'm not crazy. I'm not going to let anyone see me."

"Well, what about the beard and mustache I got for you?"

"Are you serious? That's a Santa Claus outfit. The only thing that's missing is the red suit."

"It is not. Santa's hair is white; this is like dark brown."

"He's a young Santa, then."

"Well, you're wearing it."

"No, seriously. I'm not."

"Quadir, do you understand the trouble I can get into? You're wearing the Santa face."

"Okay, I'll wear the Santa face," Quadir agreed, not wanting to bring her any trouble. In a way, she was right. If he were to be spotted alive, she would wind up in a heap of trouble.

"You'll look great."

"No, I'll look like Santa, just younger and black."

"Well, at least no one will recognize you. Come on, let's go. I got to get a quick shower and get dressed for my rounds," Amelia said as she grabbed her water bottle and threw her hand towel around her neck.

"Amelia."

"Yeah," she said, turning to face him.

"I just wanted to say thank you. Really. Thank you for everything."

"You don't have to keep saying that."

"No, I do. I really do. I just want you to know that I'm going to repay you, Amelia, for everything. I'm going to give you back all the money you've spent helping me."

"Quadir, you don't have to. I don't want your money. I have plenty of money. Really, you don't owe me anything."

"I owe you my life and I will repay you, Amelia, if it's the last thing I do on this earth. You're not the only one with money, you know," said Quadir, thinking about his hideout spot and all the millions he had stashed away safely in his safe.

"Money means very little to me, Quadir. There are far more important things in my world than money. Remember, my job is to save people's lives. Money becomes rather unimportant when you're staring at death every day."

Well, it means everything to me. Shit, I hustled too hard and got way too much paper stashed. I need to check everything out and make sure everything's safe and sound.

EYE SPY

Quadir parked the black BMW near the corner of Second and Green. He could see the door to his building. Large numbers were mounted above the door: 234. *Two-thirty-four Green Street,* he thought. *My old secret hideout.* Still in his car, he reached into a plastic bag and took out the Davy Crockett hairpieces Amelia had suggested he wear. He carefully put them on, pressing the sticky backs to his skin. He checked his mustache and beard in the rearview mirror, making sure they were on straight, and reached into the backseat for a baseball cap to put on his head. Feeling safe and undetectable, he got out of the car and walked to the front entrance of the apartment building. *I need my keys.* He wished he had his diamond Q keychain.

Just then a locksmith carrying a small duffel bag and a locked metal box brushed past him. Quadir couldn't help but notice the man's smile.

"Excuse me, I'm locked out of my house and I was just wo—"

"Sorry, pal, I can't help you right now. I'm uuhh . . . I'm off!"

Quadir watched as the man got into a locksmith van and pulled away from the block.

"Thanks a lot," said Quadir.

It turned out that the locksmith was the same one who Gena had called to open the safe. The duffel bag the locksmith was holding had his money in it, and the reason the locksmith couldn't help him was that he was in a rush to get home and share his good fortune with his wife and kids.

Quadir walked around the side of the apartment building and looked up at his old bedroom window. *That's what I'll do. I'll call the management office and have them come down here and let me in. Oh, damn, I can't do that with this Davy Crockett getup. They won't recognize me. Shit, maybe I should call a locksmith.* Quadir had to see his apartment, and he desperately needed to know that all its contents were safe and sound, especially his money.

He got back into the BMW, started the engine, and no sooner had he put the car in park than he saw her. It was Gena. She was right there in front of him, fewer than two hundred feet away, carrying a large gold-framed photo of them that had hung on the wall of his apartment. She placed it in the car. *Wow! She found my hideout spot,* he thought to himself. He watched her as she placed two pillowcases inside the car. *Is that my money in those pillowcases? What should I do?* His first thought was to jump out of the car and run over to her. That he didn't would be the biggest mistake he'd ever make. That one opportunity, that one chance was right there, but instead, he stalled, and those few moments cost him dearly. Before he knew it, the lights of the baby-blue Mercedes reflected off the car in front of it and the driver maneuvered her way out of the parking space. Quadir stepped on the gas, following the car down the street.

Where the hell is she going? he wondered as Gena made her way out of the city and onto the New Jersey Turnpike heading north. He speeded up, not wanting to lose her in the sea of red brake lights. Catching him off-guard, she quickly exited the turnpike. He cut off the car in front of him, almost causing a rear-end collision, and made the exit ramp just in the nick of time. He paid the toll and followed Gena's baby-blue Mercedes into an Exxon station off the highway. His gut instinct was to jump out of the car and run over to her, tell her that he was alive and that everything would be okay. *Yeah, that's what I'll do; I'll tell her. I'll tell her right now.* And just as he was about to get out of his car, he saw the glass door to the mobile station open, and Jerrell Jackson, his archenemy, stood in the doorway, staring straight at the BMW. Quickly, he turned on the car's engine and watched as Jerrell walked across the gas station lot, heading toward him. He quickly turned the car around and sped from the gas station. *What the fuck is she doing talking to him?* Quadir's mind wandered in all directions searching for possible explanations, but nothing made sense. *Isn't he supposed to be in jail? Forty testified and they still found that nigga not guilty?* He couldn't believe it, nothing was making sense, and worst of all was his money. It was no longer in its safe hiding place. *What is she thinking? What the hell is she thinking? She was in on this with him? She got my money for him?*

Quadir didn't know what to do. He had lost her trail and couldn't follow her anymore. He didn't want to return to Amelia's house, at least not yet. What he really wanted to do was visit his old neighborhood. Ride down the streets that he had built an empire hustling on. The streets he once owned. The streets that made him "that nigga." The streets he hadn't seen since the attempt on his life. That's what he wanted to do and that's what he was going to do. *No one can recognize me anyway.* He couldn't help it. He saw her with the pillow-cases and the picture and knew she had found his money. He drove through the streets of Philly hoping that no one would notice him. He knew he was asking for trouble coming to this side of town. *I hope the police don't pull me over.* Boy oh boy, he definitely couldn't let that happen. *No way, Jose,* he thought.

He drove down North Philly across Twenty-ninth Street over to Lehigh Avenue. Then he went down Lehigh to Seventeenth Street and took Seventeenth Street all the way up to Erie Avenue, then Erie over to Broad and back down. The streets were so familiar it all seemed like yesterday. But it wasn't yesterday and things had somehow changed over the last six months. He thought of Gena and wondered where she was. Still on Broad, he took it down to Girard and crossed over to Thirteenth and took it down to Wallace, entering Richard Allen. He had hoped to see Gena's baby-blue Mercedes parked in front of her grandmother's house, but it wasn't. He rode around the block a few times but he didn't see the car. He looked down at the time clock display in the BMW. *It's getting late.* Quadir decided it was time to go back to Amelia's house. *I'll be back, first thing in the morning. We'll see what you're up to then.*

The next morning, Quadir was again waiting outside Gena's grandmother's house. He followed her to a mall, maneuvered the BMW into a parking space just across the street from a Porsche dealership, and sat quietly and watched. Gena had started her day rather early. Had he gotten to Richard Allen a minute later, he would have missed her. As soon as the mall opened, she was the first one through the doorway. Quadir watched her as she loaded up the Mercedes with shopping bag after shopping bag. Then she went down Jewelers' Row. *No telling how much damage she did at the jewelry store. She looks happy though. She don't look like she misses me at all.* Watching Gena, he couldn't help but wonder what in the world she was thinking. She was like a madwoman with money and she was spending it and spending it big. He looked across the street at an unmarked police car and watched the detectives inside. It seemed Gena's start wasn't that early; she had company. Quadir watched as the detectives snacked on bagels and their morning coffee. He wished he could get out of the car and go to her. He wanted so bad to rush to her, to embrace her, and to tell her that he was alive and kicking. But to do that would have been too dangerous. Those extra eyes watching her would then be watching him, and he definitely didn't want that. Instead, Quadir lay low and stayed out of sight. He had no time for the Philly PD or whoever those guys were. *Maybe they're following her, hoping that she'll lead them to me.* That was his first thought, but then he thought again. *Maybe they know about the money and they're hoping that she'll lead them to it.* It could be anything, but one thing was for sure: She was definitely under surveillance. He knew he would have to keep his distance if his plan was to have any chance of success. He couldn't even get close enough to Gena to warn her.

The fact that Gena had found his money certainly complicated things. Now she was being watched. *How the hell am I gonna follow her, if ola is on her ass? How the hell will I ever get my money back?* His plan was simple: Follow Gena until she led him to his pot of gold. But now they had company and Gena was moving around a lot. She was all over the place. He couldn't afford to let the Philly PD catch him following Gena. Not those jokers—that would be a nightmare. *I bet it's a hefty sentence for faking your death.* Not to mention that Quadir certainly had not come this far to end up behind bars. The plan was the Bahamas, not the pen. He would have to shadow Gena carefully and he would have to do his best to keep her safe from a distance. *But how?*

Gena exited the Porsche dealership and stood patiently by the front door. Soon, it became evident what she was waiting for. A saleswoman pulled up in a guardsman black 911 Gemballa convertible.

"Holy shit, she's fuckin' nuts!" Quadir exclaimed. "Don't do it, Gena. They're watching you; don't do it!"

He watched from across the street as the Philly PD pulled out surveillance cameras. Gena finished with the saleswoman, shook her hand, then pulled out of the dealership parking lot. She had just blown over three hundred thousand dollars of his money and it wasn't even lunch time.

Several weeks later Quadir sat on the sofa silently as he pictured himself flipping over the coffee table and the stacks of medical journals lying on it.

"Dammit!" he muttered as he moved away from the table before he could actually trash it.

"What? What's the matter with you?" Amelia calmly asked.

Quadir looked at her, not even wanting to explain. "I can't talk about it right now."

"Talk about what?"

"Nothing. Please, not right now, Amelia."

He looked at her smile slowly fade. He had hurt her feelings and he knew it. Her entire mission in life was to help, to save, to be a hero. He completely understood that, but there was no way in the world she could help him. No one could.

"Why don't you sit down, Quadir? Just take it easy and get your thoughts together."

"Gena is seeing someone," he said.

"Gena? Your Gena? No way," said Amelia surprised at his accusation.

"Not only is she seeing someone else, she's seeing the guy that tried to kill me. His name is Jerrell Jackson."

"Oh, my god, Quadir, are you sure? That doesn't make sense. Does she know he tried to kill you?"

"I don't know what she knows, but even still, the streets is always talking and everybody knows that Jerrell was behind my murder. Everybody. What the fuck is wrong with her?"

That's when Quadir's vision came to life. Amelia sat calmly as her coffee table was flipped over and knocked to the floor, while her medical journals landed all over her living room.

"Are you done? Because tearing my things up isn't going to fix the problem, and it certainly won't help," said Amelia, turning over her coffee table and positioning it perfectly back in place.

"Yo, don't you hear me? This bitch is sleeping with the motherfucker who tried to kill me. And that's only the half of it. Gena found my money, so she's got it, all of it, and I can't figure out how to get it back. I can't even figure out where she's got it at."

"Maybe she doesn't know Jerrell shot you. And obviously she has your money because it was made available to her to get," Amelia said as she gathered her journals off the floor and began stacking them back neatly on the coffee table.

"She might not know who he is, but trust me, he knows who she is and if he thinks for one minute that she's got my money, he'll kill her for it. I know him; I know how he thinks. Every nigga I know and trusted would bring me harm if they could get their hands on that kind of money. I never let anyone know about the money I had saved. No one knew."

"Quadir, it's just money."

"You always say that, Amelia, just because you come from a well-to-do family, but twenty million ain't nothing to sneeze at."

"Twenty million? You got twenty million?"

"Do I? Well, I did. Now Gena has twenty million, or better yet, my archenemy Jerrell Jackson has twenty million."

"Oh, Quadir, twenty million?"

"Well, technically, a little over seventeen million, Amelia. And she's spending it, like water running out of a faucet."

"Well, what are you going to do? Quadir, twenty million is a lot of money."

"Amelia, please, you're making my head hurt," said Quadir, scratching his head trying to figure out his next move.

"What makes you think that if you can't figure out where the money is, Jerrell will? I'm sure Gena's not that gullible. I'm sure she's smart enough to hide the money in a safe place."

"Amelia, Jerrell is the grimiest dirtbag I know. If he thinks Gena has something, he'll torture her to death in order to take it. This shit is crazy. It's getting more and more complicated as time goes by. Now, I have to babysit this nigga."

"Listen, I have money. I can make you a loan; I can help you get a new start out here, if that's what you want. I mean I don't have twenty million dollars and I know that's a lot of money, but Quadir, it's not worth your life. It's not worth prison. You know what I'm saying?" asked Amelia, hoping he was smarter than she thought.

"Amelia, a loan? Are you nuts? We're talking my twenty million, Amelia, my twenty million dollars, and I will get my money back. I have to get it back!"

"No, we're talking about Gena's twenty million and we're talking about you risking your life!" she shouted, hoping to penetrate his brain with common sense.

Quadir just looked at her blankly, not wanting to hear her logic. "That's my twenty million. Mine. I busted my ass for that; I damn near lost my life for that. I want my money. I want it back!"

"Well, what do you want me to do to help? What about hiring a private investigator to help track the money down?"

"No, that would just be one more nose up in the mix. Shit, he'd probably find out where the money is and take it himself."

"Quadir!"

"What? I would," he said, eyes wide.

"Can I ask you a question?"

"Yeah, what?" he asked, stopping his pacing for a split second to hear her out.

"Are you mad at Gena for having your money or are you mad at her for being with Jerrell?"

Quadir thought about her question and honestly didn't

know the answer. His pride was hurt, of course. Any man's pride would be. That was just the tip of the iceberg. The truth was his archenemy had his girl and access to his dough. Nothing could be worse than that.

"Right now, I just want my money back," he said, brokenhearted.

"She thinks you're dead, you know," said Amelia, trying to reason with him.

"I know, but he's the enemy."

"She probably has no idea who she's dealing with."

Quadir just shook his head. The situation was way out of control. *Why didn't I stop her at the apartment? Why didn't I stop her then, before she had a chance to get into the car? What was I thinking?*

"Damn, I want my money."

Amelia said nothing; she just let him pace around, scratching his head, hoping he'd figure out something without harming himself or, worse, her medical career. Of course he knew that to do something foolish would just be plain stupid. He had everything going for him: a new life, a fresh start, and twenty million dollars somewhere out there. And he would figure out where. He had come too far not to. He would have his money. He might not have Gena, but he'd get that money back, one way or the other. *What are you doing, Gena? Of all the dudes out here, why him?* Gena had committed the perfect betrayal. If Quadir didn't know any better, he'd swear she was in cahoots with Jerrell. *No, she loved me, didn't she?*

"Are you okay?" Amelia asked, lightly touching Quadir's shoulder.

"No, I'm not. I'm really not."

"Seriously, let me hire someone to help you get your money back."

"Not yet; not right now. She already has Philly PD on her, and if you hire a PI then it'll look like a damn caravan going down the street. I just need to change up my tactics and I need to switch cars too."

"You can use the Jeep, if you want," said Amelia, hoping to be helpful. "Just be careful."

"I will; don't worry."

"Quadir, don't you worry. She'll be back."

Quadir thought for a moment, and the truth was that after he saw Gena and Jerrell together, he didn't know if he wanted her back.

She'll be back? Maybe she should stay where she's at; maybe she don't need to come back.

Amelia strolled out of the room while Quadir contemplated his next move. He would switch cars and push the Range and he would change up his hours. She was hiding the money somewhere and sooner or later she would lead him to it. Either that or Jerrell would, but one way or the other he was going to watch her like a hawk. And watch out for those snooping detective motherfuckers too! *I wonder if they're FBI.*

"Doc!" he hollered as she walked by the living room and into the dining room.

"Yeah, what's up?" she asked leaning backward in the doorway.

"Thanks," said Quadir.

"Don't thank me; I'm just waiting to see this twenty million dollars. Maybe I *will* let you pay me back," she said, laughing.

"I thought you said money could never repay what you had done for me," said Quadir, trying to match his voice to hers.

"Are you nuts? Twenty million . . . I'm ready to go out there with you and follow Gena around myself. She's lucky I got rounds to make or I'd be out there with you. Now, you said you needed the Jeep, right?"

SPARKLES

That night when Quadir returned to Amelia's he found her in the kitchen preparing what appeared to be a gourmet homemade meal.

"Wow, I didn't know you knew how to cook."

"Yup, it's true; you learn something new about a person every day. See, you never know, right?"

"I know I'm hungry."

"Yeah, well, be patient. This is very serious food I'm preparing. So, how did it go tonight, private eye?"

"Well, it went. From what I could see, she's definitely fallen for Jerrell, that's for sure. She went back to his place. I stayed outside until . . ."

"Until what?"

"Until they turned the lights off."

"Quadir, I'm so sorry," said Amelia, as she stopped draining linguini long enough to see the hurt in his face.

"Hey, I guess that's life. You know, sometimes you win and sometimes you lose."

"Yeah, but sometimes you lose, and you also win, you know?"

"No, I don't."

"Well, like right now, you feel like you lost, but Quadir, you're on top, you're alive, you have the upper hand, and most of all, you know what's going on around you. Gena might not know, but you do."

"How will I get my money back?"

"Now that, I don't know. Have you ever thought of just simply asking her for it?"

"Yeah, but now that's she's with Jerrell, I don't want her to see me. I'd rather her just think I'm dead."

Amelia looked at Quadir as he lowered his head. She understood how he felt and wanted to do whatever she could to make him feel better. But the truth was, there was nothing anyone could do that would make him feel better.

"Hey, want to play cards?"

"I don't much feel like playing cards."

"Well, let's eat; dinner's ready."

After dinner Amelia cleaned up the kitchen and loaded the dirty dishes into the dishwasher. Quadir retired to the living room where he turned on the news. He sat on the sofa where he fell asleep.

Just then, Gena knocked at the door. Amelia entered the living room and let Quadir know she was there.

"Let her in."

Gena walked into the living room where Quadir was. Their eyes met and Quadir took her hands into his. "I love you."

"I love you, too, Quadir. I'm so glad you're okay. Now we can be together."

Quadir took her into his arms and caressed the back of her

neck, cradling her head in the palm of his hand. He kissed her mouth ever so gently. Their lips locked as they had so long ago. At that moment Quadir realized it was Amelia he was holding and not Gena.

"I want you, Quadir; I want to be with you."

"Amelia, there's no turning back. You understand? No turning back."

"I understand," she said.

In her heart she knew exactly what he was saying. There was no turning back. There was only the forward motion of them together.

Their lips locked tightly as Quadir moved, swiftly covering her body with his. His hands pulled up her shirt as his fingers caressed her breasts. With each breath he took, she breathed in unison, and she could feel his hard penis through his clothing pressing against her mound. He moved his hand down to her pants and unbuttoned them, pulling them down, freeing one leg at a time. How he had gotten his clothes off was beyond her; all Amelia knew was that she was ready. Ready to be with him, ready to make love to him, and ready to be loved by him. There was nothing she wouldn't do for him, nothing. She had already proven that by saving his life, and risking her career by faking his death.

They made love for hours and when they were done it was as if the memory of Gena had been completely erased. The only thing on his mind was how he was going to get his money back.

Maybe Amelia is right; maybe I should just ask her for it.

Rik hurried into the restaurant, closing his umbrella at the door. The weather outside was beyond dreadful. Rain fell from the sky like a monsoon. Rik took off his raincoat, folded it over his arm, and walked to the maître d'.

"Table for one, sir?" she asked.

"No, I'm with the Santero party."

"Oh, he's already here. I just showed him in a minute ago." The hostess grabbed a menu and started for the table. "Follow me, please, and I'll show you to your table."

She led Rik to the table where his dinner guest was waiting.

"Rik, what's happening, my man?" Tony rose and embraced him tightly. "Here, have a seat."

Rik took the seat across from Tony.

"Have the waitress bring us a bottle of your finest wine, please," Tony told the maître d'. He waited until she departed and then took his seat again. "Rik, my man, how are you?"

Rik shook his head. "Not good, Tony. Not too good."

Tony waved him off. "We'll make it all better, my man."

"I don't know."

"Don't worry. Just wait until you hear the proposal we have for you."

The waitress arrived with the wine and two glasses. "Are you ready to order, sir?"

"What would you like to eat, Rik?" Tony asked.

Rik shrugged. "Um, let me do the filet, medium well, butterfly cut, with the creamed spinach and mashed potatoes. And, also, let me get a Caesar salad to start."

"And for you, sir?" the waitress asked Tony.

"You know what, I'll have the filet well done, butterfly cut, but Oscar that with a side of the sweet potato casserole, please. And I'll take a Caesar salad also."

"Very well, sir." The waitress nodded, removed the menus from the table, and disappeared.

"Here is what we have in mind," Tony continued. "Twenty keys a week. We front you half, you pay for the other half up front. You don't have to pay for the front until the following week when we drop you off another ten."

"Damn. That's sweet."

Tony smiled. "I told you we'd take good care of you."

"Good, because I'ma need a little help."

Tony lifted an eyebrow. "What kinda help?"

"I'ma need an extension on what I owe you."

Tony recoiled. "An extension? What kinda extension?"

"Well, really, I was hoping that you could spot me some dope, and let me work off what I owe you."

"Work off what you owe us? Are you telling me that you don't have the money, Rik?"

"I got busted, Tony. You already know this. The cops hit my stash house and found the shit."

Tony looked down and shook his head gravely. "That's not our problem, Rik. You know how we operate."

"Man, that shit was beyond my control. I got busted. Man, c'mon."

"Rik, I know the way my uncle thinks. His first question is going to be, if the cops found the dope, then why are you out on the streets? That's a question that you don't want him to ask. Because he's not going to understand all of the legal tech-nicalities involved. The first thing that is going to come to his mind is that you've rolled over. And that would be something that would be very bad for you."

"I didn't roll over; you know that. I would never do nothing like that. They threw the case out because the snitch turned up dead."

"But you're saying that they found the dope."

"Yeah, in a house rented under a fake name. They couldn't trace it back to me; they just knew that me and the homeboys met there sometimes. That's what got the house raided. But they couldn't put the dope on any specific individual."

Tony smiled. "Rik, my uncle's old school. He ain't gonna understand all of that legal mumbo jumbo bullshit. He's gonna want his money, or he's gonna want you in prison because of that dope, or he's gonna want you dead."

"Man, I'm not trying to fuck over anybody. I just need more time, and some more work to get it all back to you."

"Do you hear yourself? You're asking for more work, without paying us for the work we've already given you. After you're telling us that you got busted with that previous work, but you're still out on the streets. Do you hear this shit?"

"You know it's true."

"Rik, we are men, aren't we? Let's talk like men. Because there is much truth that you speak, and I believe you, Rik. If I didn't, we wouldn't be sitting here. But this is the problem, Rik. Quadir fronted you a lot of product before he was killed. Do you remember that?"

Rik thought quietly for a moment, knowing exactly where Tony was going with his conversation.

"And for what I know, Quadir passed to you at least two hundred keys, my friend, at least that much, maybe more. And you paid little to nothing back. Quadir died and you walked with all that coke and all that money. Rik, now you have nothing. Wow, my friend, you had it all. You had it all." Tony exhaled and shook his head. "Here's what I'm going to do. I'm going to pretend like we never had this conversation. I'm going to pretend like I haven't gotten around to picking up the money that you owe us. I'm going to stall, and try to buy you a little time. In the meantime, I suggest you do whatever the hell it is that you need to do to come up with that money. My uncle is not going to understand. If I can't collect from you after a certain period of time, he's going to send a fucking hit squad over to wipe the streets up with your ass; it's nothing personal, just business. Get the money."

Tony rose, pulled out a wad of money, and threw several hundred-dollar bills onto the table. "Enjoy the meal. Then go home and get some rest. You look like shit."

Rik lowered his head into his palms as Tony disappeared.

He knew that he had to come up with the money, and he knew that Tony was serious about what his uncle would do if he didn't. He just needed time. A little bit of time, and a little bit of dope to work. He could hit the streets and make miracles happen, if only he had a little bit to work with.

Rik scratched his head. Truth be told, he didn't know how much time he had. *I wonder how long Tony can stall his uncle. Even if I had some coke, I might not have the time I need to flip it. No, I definitely need to pay Tony. But how? I need some major coins to build my stash back up and get the Santeros off my ass.* Rik knew that he would have to dust off his pistol and jack someone. *Damn, who's holding these days that I might stick?* Most ballers like that had an entourage and bodyguards. And none of them would let him borrow that kind of dough. *Hold up; wait a minute.* A light suddenly went off in his brain. Actually, he did know someone who would let him borrow that kind of dough. She had offered it to him once before. There

was no doubt that she would offer it again. *Gena; she's holdin'*
all Quadir's loot. She's the one, the missing piece to my puzzle.

Rik sat back and smiled as the waitress delivered his meal.
Everything was going to be all right. He knew exactly where to
get the money from to get those fucking Barranquilla Colom-
bians off his back. The only question was how he would get it.
Should I just ask her or should I just jack her?

RESURRECTED

Gena listened as Quadir finished his story. Still dazed and unable to believe that Quadir was alive, Gena couldn't help but think about the series of unfortunate events. Meeting Jerrell at that gas station was the worst thing that could have happened. What was worse was that he was Quadir's enemy, the one behind killing her beloved Quadir. He was nothing more than a monster. *How could I have been so stupid?* Gena couldn't help but blame herself. Just then she thought of the baby she was carrying—Jerrell's baby. *Quadir must not ever know that I'm pregnant. What will I do?*

"So, you've been staying here, getting well?"

"Yes. Amelia brought me here after I was released from the inpatient rehabilitation center at the hospital. Now, I have physical therapy here and I go to outpatient treatment."

"And Amelia, where is she?"

"She's at work. She's always at the hospital."

"So, you said that you and her became involved after you saw me and Jerrell together."

"Gina, listen . . ."

"No, Quadir, please, just answer me. You are involved with her, right?"

Quadir was silent, trying to figure out her angle. He honestly didn't understand her line of questioning, but the look on her face told it all. Her entire world had crashed all around her the night he died. Now, it would crash again when she learned that he was not only alive, but also in love with someone else.

"Answer me, please. Please tell me the truth, please."

"Yes, Gena, yes. I love her."

"You love her?" Gena asked, as tears began to stream down her face. She broke down, seating herself gently on the end of an ottoman that was next to a chair. "I don't understand, I just don't understand. Why, Quadir, why? Why'd you do this to me? Why? I thought you loved me, please, I would have never been with Jerrell. I didn't know who he was, please, Quadir. I don't know what to say," Gena said, trying with all her might to hold back the tears that just seemed to flow down her cheeks. She wanted to be strong; she wanted to have an ounce of pride. But she had none. The man she adored and loved more than life itself was standing there confessing that he was in love with someone else.

"I mean, what is there really left to say? You and Jerrell were together, or at least you were with him," said Quadir, full of frustration.

"Oh, my God, I can't believe what you're saying. I just can't. It can't be this way. It's not supposed to be this way, no," she said, freaking out, shaking her hands in the air, trying to find the reason for everything that was happening.

"Gena, please calm down . . ."

"No, don't tell me to calm down. You were dead, Quadir, gone. Why would your mother throw me out like that, if . . . did she know?"

Quadir stood still, knowing what his mother had done.

"Listen, Gena, my moms did what she had to do. She was only trying to protect me."

"Protect you? Protect you? Are you serious? That's your answer? You just let her throw me out like that, with nothing. You left me with nothing. You died, and now you're back, but you're back and you don't want me anymore because of Jerrell, and I can understand that. I can understand it all. I see it all real clear. Fuck me, right? Fuck me, right, Quadir?" she yelled at the top of her lungs, ready to break something.

"Gena, please, it's not like that. It's not like that, really."

"Then what could it possibly be like?"

"You don't understand; you're too emotional to understand right now . . ."

"Please, Quadir, please, just leave me alone," said Gena. They both stood in silence as Amelia's BMW pulled into the driveway. The garage door opened and then they heard it close.

"I guess that's her. Amelia, the most fabulous doctor in the world. The doctor who brings people back from the dead. Wow, she must be something, really something. Not only does she save her patients, she fucks them too," said Gena as she began to make her way back to her room.

"Gena, wait, listen . . . Please, Gena, there's something I need to tell you; please listen to me, it's important." Quadir followed her as she slammed the guest bedroom door in his face.

"Tell it to yourself!" Gena screamed, opening the door.

"No, better yet, tell Amelia," she said, slamming the door in his face again.

She ran over to the phone on the nightstand and called a yellow cab.

"Hello, yes, ma'am, I need a taxi." *Fuck, I don't even know where the hell I'm at.* "Never mind," she said, hanging up the phone.

Gena searched the room quickly for her clothes. She dressed, quietly crept down the stairs, and climbed out an open window in the library. She snuck away before Quadir and Amelia knew she was gone.

Terrell walked briskly through the park, trying to make it to his meeting place and wrap things up before the rain started coming down again. He hated the weather this time of year, especially when it got locked in a rainy cycle. It was one of the reasons he had left the city. He hated the rain, and even more so, he despised the cold. The weather in his new city was as different from this shit as night and day. He had relocated to beautiful, sunny South Florida, and he loved it. He had vowed never to set foot in the city of brotherly love again, but now, business had forced him to come back. He had flown in to avenge his younger brother.

Champagne pulled up to the park in her black S600 and backed into a parking space. She hated meeting Terrell; he was worse than his twin brother. At least Jerrell had a little bit of sense about him, even a little bit of class, compared with Terrell. They were both cold, heartless men, but Terrell was a straight-up animal. He was a brute, with no sense of social grace, no understanding, no limitations, no nothing. He followed his most basic instincts, as if he were a hyena or lion or some other wild-ass animal. The bad part about Terrell was his attitude. The penal system ate him up a long time ago and even though he had not been locked up for more than fifteen years, he still had an institutionalized mentality. He didn't give a fuck and he didn't care. He never would, just like most men who served time.

Champagne could see him in the distance, standing and waiting for her. Goosebumps covered her body, and she felt creepy, crawling creatures up and down her spine. It was a feeling she got whenever she was around Terrell. She hated the way he looked at her, the way he stared at her body. He really was the worst. Champagne knew if he ever got the chance to sex her, he would. And she had no doubt that he would be as brutal as possible while doing it. Jerrell had told her plenty of stories about his brother. Terrell liked to take pussy. Jerrell never understood why the women didn't press charges. Some would end up with black eyes and bruised bodies. But no one ever pressed charges. Jerrell figured the women were too scared. Either that or they had such scandalous pasts that the charges would never stick and they would just end up looking like the whores they truly were.

Champagne looked at the sick, twisted grin spread across Terrell's face. She could picture him beating the shit out of her, raping her, and then sadistically burning her body inside some giant cathedral or something. He was just a fucking weird, deranged, serial killer type, waiting to be set off— probably from the simplest of things, such as saying the wrong word, like "bananas."

Champagne walked to the center of the park where Terrell was standing and waiting. He pulled her close and hugged her.

She could feel his hand sliding down to her ass as his fingers reached between her legs.

"Hey, motherfucker, slow down!" Champagne shoved him away.

"I'm grieving and distraught, and this is how you treat me?" Terrell asked.

"Not distraught enough where you can't grip a handful of ass though, huh?"

Terrell smiled. "People grieve in different ways."

"Don't put your filthy hands on me again," Champagne ordered him.

Terrell raised his hands in surrender.

Champagne stared at him in silence for several moments before exhaling. "So, you all right?"

"Fuck no, my brother's dead."

"I'm sorry, you know. I'm sorry for your family."

Terrell shrugged her emotions away. "What do you have for me?" he asked as he let his eyes roam down her body and stared between her legs.

Champagne shook her head. "Never that. Don't ever even think about that!"

Terrell smiled again and looked up at her.

Champagne opened her Louis Vuitton handbag and pulled out a photo. "This is the chick he was fucking with. He had me check up on her before he got shot up. I have no doubt he was with her when it happened. Her name is Gena Scott."

"She set him up?"

Champagne shrugged. "Only he or she could tell you that. I wasn't there. But one thing's for certain, she ain't no innocent bitch. She's down for fucking with a baller, so she could have set J up."

"Tell me everything you know about this bitch."

"She's from Richard Allen. She lives with her grandmother; some old bitch they call Gah Git. She was fucking with the boy Quadir real strong until he got killed and, rumor has it, your brother was behind his murder, so it's very well possible that Gena sought revenge against Jerrell for Quadir, or at least that's what some people are saying. Who knows what makes people tick, you know?"

"So, she could have been setting my brother up all along to get revenge for her nigga, Quadir."

Champagne shrugged. "I don't know, but it does make a lot of sense. But only he or she could tell you that."

Terrell took the picture and examined it carefully. "I can find this bitch in Richard Allen?"

"Richard Allen wouldn't be a bad place to start. That's where she's from and it's where her family lives."

Terrell examined Gena's picture. Blood rushed to his face as it became twisted in a dark mask of pure evil. He was staring at the bitch who had set his brother up. *This the bitch that was playing you, little bro, misleading you, smiling in your face and shit; don't worry, I got you. I know she probably gave you the pussy just to throw you off, all so she could get even for her man. Mmm-hmm, I see you, bitch.* He couldn't help thinking to himself of all the things he planned to do to Gena. He decided right then and there that he was going to fuck her. He was going to tie her up and torture her, and fuck her in places that she never knew she could be fucked. He was going to make her beg him to kill her. She would plead with him to end her pain, end her life, end her miserable suffering. He was going to do things to her that he had never done to anyone else before. And he had done so much to so many people in his lifetime. But this one—this one was going to be special.

Champagne saw the look on Terrell's face and began to panic. His face was set in a deep scowl, and his eyes had become red and glazed over. The nigga looked like he was about to explode.

Champagne backed away from him. "You can keep the picture."

Terrell seemed to not even notice her leaving. He was too deep in thought of all the things he planned to do to seek his revenge against Gena.

Once Champagne was a safe distance away, she turned and hurried to her car. *Bitch, ain't you glad you didn't say "bananas"!*

Lieutenant Mark Ratzinger lifted his hand calling for a round of beer. The bartender nodded, and Mark turned back to his associates.

"Where are we at on this?" Ratzinger asked.

"We're tracking her." Dick Davis told him. "She's made some big purchases, but she hasn't led us to the money yet."

Letoya Ellington shrugged. "She's smarter than we thought. She must've kept an extremely large sum out to spend. The rest, she must've hid. And besides the car, and some jewelry, she hasn't really spent big."

"She could not touch that stash for months," Dick added. "Hell, maybe even years."

Ratzinger shook his head. "Well, it's getter harder and harder to justify the money and man hours we're spending tracking her. Pretty soon, somebody is gonna wanna know why we're on her, and why we haven't produced anything."

Cornell Cleaver nodded. "He's right, guys. This thing can't go on too much longer. We're going to have to come up with something, and soon."

"Like what?" Ellington asked.

Ratzinger shrugged. "Is she dirty in any kinda way? Can we swoop on her and press her?"

The drinks arrived at the table. The detectives sat in silence as the waitress passed their beers around the table. The conversation resumed as soon as she left.

"As far as we can tell?" Ellington shook her head. "Other than spending drug money, no. She's clean."

"Can we plant something on her, bring her in, and then pressure her?" Cleaver asked.

Ratzinger shook his head. "That means we would have to bring in a black and white."

"So? There's enough money to go around." Cleaver replied.

"The fewer people we have involved in this, the better," Ratzinger told him.

"I'm Internal Affairs. I can get us a couple of dirty patrolmen to pull her ass over and plant the shit. That's nothing; we do it every day," Cleaver told them.

"I can break her in the confession room," Ellington added.

"Break her? She hasn't committed a crime. Police 101, guys, remember your first day at the academy. An innocent person isn't going to confess," Ratzinger pointed out.

Cleaver leaned forward. "I say we get her in the room, let her know how much time she's facing, and we get her to trade her freedom for the goddamn money."

"And if she doesn't confess?" Ratzinger asked. "What if she doesn't break? What if she requests an attorney? What if some hotshot lawyer walks her ass out of the station and is on the phone with Internal Affairs the next day? What happens then? Anybody thought about that shit? Jesus Christ, guys! Think! We can do better than that shit!"

Davis leaned back in his chair. "What about a boyfriend? You think she'd give it up to a lover?"

Ellington smiled. "I don't think you're her type, Dickie."

"Not me, asshole. I'm talking about bringing in a young detective friend of mine to seduce her ass."

"And you think he looks hot enough to seduce her?" Ellington laughed. "Dickie, I'm going to have to watch you."

"Fuck you, Toya!" Davies groped himself. "This is all dick, and it loves nothing but pussy."

"Okay, at least you guys are thinking," Ratzinger told them.

"Hey what about the big fish you caught, what was that guy's name, umm . . . Rick or Rik," Cleaver said. "What about him?"

Ellington shrugged. "What about him?"

"She offered to help him once, didn't she? Maybe she'd be willing to offer it to him again."

Ellington nodded. "Maybe."

"We just have to make him need it." Davis smiled.

"We'll bust his ass, as soon as he jaywalks." Cleaver added. "We can plant some shit on him, juice things up for the judge so his bond is through the roof, and put the word out on the street."

"How can we guarantee that she'll get the word, or even give a shit?" Davis asked. "And how can we be sure that she'll even make the offer again, or that he'll accept it?"

"Look, we just need to come up with a way to get her to

lead us to wherever she's got it stashed," Ratzinger told them. "What about the grandmother? Any medical bills? Any creditors? Anybody close to her that she would loan a large sum of money to? That's what we need to start looking for, see who she's close to. Start tracking friends and family. See who she hangs out with and calls all the time. Real police work, ladies and gentlemen, time to show why each of you made detective."

Ellington lifted her beer into the air. "To making detective."

"Detective!" The others lifted their glasses to toast.

"Let's hurry up and put this bitch in the poorhouse," Cleaver added.

The others around the table laughed.

MANHUNT

Terrell walked to the door and pounded on it forcefully. He hated being in Richard Allen, especially on a day like today, when he had business to take care of. There was always some stupid-ass niggas wanting to stare you down or eyeball you like they're hard. And when you played the game with them, it almost always led to a gunfight. He had no time for that kind of bullshit today. No, today he was on a mission. He needed to handle his business and keep it moving. Gah Git opened the front door.

"May I help you?" she asked.

"I'm looking for her." Terrell held up the photo that he had of Gena.

"Her?" Gah Git eyed him suspiciously. "I don't know who that is."

"Your granddaughter."

"I don't have my glasses on. You got a name?"

Terrell smiled. "Gena. I'm looking for Gena."

"Oh, well, Gena don't live here no more. What's your

name? If she calls I'll tell her you came by. If you want you can leave me your phone number for her."

"I heard that she does live here."

"Well, you heard wrong, son."

"You wouldn't be trying to play games with me, would you?" Terrell asked. "She's not inside hiding or anything like that, right?"

"Who the hell do you think you're talking to? Now, I said she ain't here and she don't live here, and don't you come back here no more," Gah Git said, trying to slam the door in his face, but Terrell stuck his foot in the door.

"What the hell are you doing?" Gah Git shouted. "Gary! Gary!"

Terrell shoved the door open, knocking Gah Git onto the floor. He stepped inside and closed the door behind him.

"Get the hell outta my house!" Gah Git shouted. "Gary!"

Gary ran down the stairs. "What the fuck is going on?" He leaned forward and helped his grandmother up. "Who the fuck are you?"

"Where's Gena?" Terrell demanded. "Is she here?"

"Nigga, you better get the fuck outta here!" Gary told him.

Terrell shoved Gary out of the way and walked into the kitchen.

"Nigga, I said get the fuck outta my grandmom's house!" Gary shouted. He charged Terrell.

Terrell backhanded Gary, and then clasped his hand around Gary's throat. Gary gripped Terrell's hand and struggled to free himself. Terrell tossed Gary aside like a rag doll, sending him flying over the living-room coffee table.

"Oh, my God, Gary! Gary, you okay?" asked Gah Git, running to her grandson's side. "Get the hell outta here!" Gah Git shouted.

Gary rose and charged Terrell again. Terrell punched Gary in his stomach, dropping him to the floor. He kicked Gary in his stomach, and then pulled out his pistol.

"I'm tired of this bullshit! Where the fuck is she?"

"Oh, my God, no, please! Oh, God, please don't kill him! Don't kill him!" Gah Git pleaded.

Terrell turned the pistol backward and struck Gah Git across her jaw. "Where the fuck is she?"

Gah Git fell to the floor again.

"Where the fuck is she?" Terrell asked, striking Gah Git with the pistol once again.

Gary tried to rise. "Leave her alone!"

Terrell struck Gah Git across her face again, and then kicked her in her stomach. Gary braced himself and stood back up to charge Terrell, but before he could, Terrell turned around with the pistol in his hand and fired a shot into Gary's stomach. "Lay down, bitch!"

Gary flew back into an end table, knocking over a lamp. Terrell turned his attention back to a crying Gah Git.

"Where is she, old woman?"

"I don't know . . ."

Terrell gripped Gah Git's hair and pulled her face up toward his. "How do you get in touch with her?"

"She just comes by!" Gah Git shouted.

Terrell struck her with the handle of his pistol several times, causing blood to pour from her head, her nose, and her mouth. "Wrong answer, old woman!"

Terrell continued to beat Gah Git with the pistol until she

was unconscious. He then began to search the apartment. Terrell tore through the place, ransacking it in the process. He searched drawers for an address or a telephone number that would lead him to Gena. He found none. By the time he returned downstairs, Gah Git was awake and dragging her bloody, beaten, and bruised body into the kitchen where the phone hung on the wall.

"Well, well, well." Terrell smiled. "Where are we going?"

"No, please . . ." Gah Git begged. "Just go. My grand-baby needs an ambulance. Please . . ."

"Call her," Terrell said sternly.

"What?"

"Pick up the goddamned telephone and call Gena!"

"I don't have her number! I swear to the good Lord, I don't have no number for that chile!"

Terrell grabbed Gah Git by her hair and bent her over the kitchen table. "When you see her, I want you to give her a message for me."

"Okay."

"Tell her I said this." Terrell lifted Gah Git's housecoat in the back and ripped off her underwear. Gah Git screamed like a wild animal, but Terrell covered her mouth as he forced himself inside her. He ravaged her violently, though what seemed to last a lifetime lasted only four minutes. Gah Git had found herself at some low times in her life, but somehow, she had always made it through. She had always found strength in her God.

Once her assailant left the apartment, Gah Git crawled up to the telephone and dialed 911. She then crawled into the living room, lifted Gary's head into her bloody lap, and talked to him to keep him from going into shock. The entire time she waited, she couldn't help but call to God. *You gonna have to carry me through this, carry me on. Why, God, why? Please don't let my grandbaby die in here today; take me, Lord, take me, but don't take my grandbaby; don't take him.*

GONNA GETCHA

Joshua Harbinger had been in the Federal Bureau of Investigations for the last eight years of his life. He had graduated from Harvard in the top of his class at the age of nineteen and had been recruited by the Bureau straight out of college. His plan had been to go to Harvard Law, but after talking to the Bureau's recruiter midway through his senior year, he caught the FBI bug.

Josh, as he was mostly called, had for the most part lived a very sheltered life. His father was the United States ambassador to Australia, and his mother was a former United States attorney, and she was also a former White House counsel. Josh grew up around privilege and power. He also grew up around money, lots of it. His maternal grandfather was a former international commodities trader who later became a United States senator, while his father's father was the founder of a very successful Wall Street brokerage. Josh was the product of the Andover prep school and had been groomed to go to Harvard

Law so he could take over the family business. He, however, craved excitement and danger.

His first years in the Bureau were spent chasing low-level counterfeiters and investigating missing children cases. Eventually, after plenty of wild and loose but lucky stunts, he worked his way up the ladder and built a reputation as a maverick who would get the job done. His reputation won him a transfer to New York to work on the high-profile organized crime leaders and the New York Mafia families. Once they had been pretty much broken up, he was transferred to Philadelphia, where he was biding his time until he made deputy special agent in charge. He wouldn't be content until he was in charge of his own major field office. He had been told that his promotion was in the works. The actual words were more along the lines of "It's basically being a done deal." All he had to do was sit tight. He, on the other hand, had other plans.

Josh knocked on the door of his boss's office. His boss was none other than Special Agent in Charge Rudy Galvani. Galvani was a no-nonsense FBI agent through and through. Born in the Bensonhurst section of Brooklyn, Galvani had been raised on the mean streets of New York. He had watched his older brother, two uncles, and several of his cousins fall victim to gang and drug violence. It was after the funeral of his cousin Manuel that he promised his mother he would keep his shit clean, and he did. As a youngster, Galvani stuck his nose into his books, and for extracurricular activities, he played football and basketball and ran track. He was something of a high-school football star. He had led his traditionally horrid football team to a ten and three season, losing in the playoffs after meeting what was destined to be the state's high-school football champions that year. So the team held its head up high, and Galvani, the star running back, was the pride of his community.

Academics took Galvani to Harvard on a scholarship. He was the first person in his family to go to college and he did it in a major way. Harvard Law followed graduation, and then an internship to a Supreme Court justice. A short stint with the Justice Department and a change of administrations found him transferring over to the Bureau. That was fifteen years ago, and now he was in charge of his own major field office. He was known in law enforcement circles as "The Hammer." He would bust his own mother if he found her doing something illegal. His reputation for being an asshole was actually something that he was proud of. He gave no quarter, and he expected none in return. That was why his relationship with Josh was a curious one. Josh was Mr. Cut Corners, while Galvani was Mr. Straight and Narrow. How they even got along was a mystery to everyone in the Bureau. Agents in the office had taken to calling them oil and water. They simply did not mix.

"In!" Galvani shouted.

Josh pushed open the door and stepped inside. "Hey, boss man!"

Galvani nodded toward the chair in front of his desk. "Have a seat."

Josh seated himself and started digging through the jar of candy on his boss's desk.

"I got your report, Josh," Galvani told him. "Do you really want to open up this can of worms? It's going to cause a shitstorm."

Josh shrugged. "I don't care. This Cleaver guy is dirty, dirtier than a prostitute's panties on a busy Saturday night."

Galvani nodded.

"He's the cancer," Josh continued. "He's rotten at the core. He's spreading his corruption throughout the department."

"You can't go after this guy with nothing more than a hunch."

"I have more than a hunch, sir. He's dirty, sir. Also, I had a peek into his file."

Galvani leaned back in his chair. "You looked into his file? How did you get access to an Internal Affairs detective's file?"

"I have this friend who works for . . ."

Galvani lifted his hand silencing him. He didn't want to know. That way if the shit hit the fan, he could say he didn't know and at least that would be the truth.

"Sir, something's off, just hear me out. Cornell Cleaver has been reassigned, investigated, reprimanded, and transferred more than any officer in the history of the department. Someone just keeps sweeping his shit under the rug. That tells me that he's probably got someone higher up looking out for him, probably just as corrupt."

Galvani shook his head. "Keep it focused, Josh. Don't worry about any higher-ups. We'll just keep them out of the loop on this one. So, how do you plan on pursuing this one?"

"I don't think going undercover is necessary."

"You want me to get you assigned to a case with this guy?"

Josh nodded. "That would be great, sir. If you could do that, I could bring this asshole down. But in the meantime, I want to do a little snooping around. I noticed that he associates only with certain officers and only one from Internal Affairs. The others are from various other departments and precincts."

"And?"

"Well, it's weird, sir. These Internal Affairs guys are pariahs. No one wants to hang with the guy charged with investigating them and possibly getting them fired or sent to prison. Yet, there's a whole clique that he is rumored to be tight with, and they're all detectives. These Internal Affairs guys usually hang together, because nobody else wants to hang with them."

"Be careful on this one, Josh. No wild and loose stunts."

Josh smiled. "I wouldn't think of it."

"I want to be kept in the loop, too. I want to know what you're up to at all times."

Josh nodded. "Will do. I'm just going to do a little snooping around and see what I can come up with."

Galvani nodded. "Good luck and happy hunting."

Josh rose. "I'm going to bag this crooked bastard and everybody down with him. You can bet your ass on this."

Galvani nodded, and Josh exited the room.

It must have taken Gena three hours before she caught a cab. She realized she was definitely in the suburbs. The neighborhood was nothing but grass, trees, and monstrous million-dollar homes. *I'll never get a cab out here.* Tired, hungry and still not 100 percent, she felt weak and faint standing on her feet. Every few minutes she would stop and rest by sitting on the curb or leaning against parked cars. Finally, she saw a cab heading up the street toward her. Thank God it stopped.

"Where to, lady?"

For a few seconds Gena didn't know where she was going. She thought quickly and then gave the cabbie instructions. Gena had the cab drop her off at the corner of her old block, at Fifty-second and Chancellor Street. She wished she still had her old apartment, but wishing would get her nowhere. Had she not moved in with Quadir, her uncle Michael would still be renting the place for her. She walked down the block unnoticed and up the steps to Markita's door. She rang the bell and waited.

"Who?"

"It's me, Gena."

"Gena, girl, everybody and they momma been calling here looking for you. Where the hell have you been? Something done happened to your grandma. They said some man attacked her and shot Gary up and he's in critical condition."

"What?" asked Gena, confused.

"Girl, it's bad; it's been on the news and everything. The police are looking for the man and everything; they got a bulletin out and his picture. You know how they do the drawings? You better call somebody. You better call home."

Gena picked up the receiver of Markita's phone and dialed her cousin Bria's cell phone. There was no answer, so Gena hung up and dialed again. On the second ring Bria answered the phone.

"Bria, it's me, Gena. What's going on?"

"Gena, some man came up in Gah Git's house looking for you. But Gah Git told him she ain't know where you was and he beat her and Gary tried to stop him, but he beat Gary then shot him in the stomach and then he . . ." her voice faded out and Gena couldn't hear her.

"And then what, what happened?"

"Then he raped Gah Git."

"What? Oh my God," said Gena, as she began to unravel.

"She's in the hospital at Temple and Gary's there too. Gena, it's bad. Aunt Paula, Uncle Michael, and Aunt Gwendolyn are all at the hospital, and they saying Gary's not gonna make it. He's on life support, Gena," said Bria as she started crying.

"Okay, okay, I'm on my way. I'm on my way!" said Gena, before placing the phone in its cradle.

"What happened?" Markita asked.

"It's just like you said, Gah Git and Gary is in the hospital. Some man went to Gah Git's house looking for me. He beat Gary and shot him and beat Gah Git and raped her."

"Oh, my God, Gena, no!"

"That's just the half of it," said Gena, thinking of Quadir. She wished she could tell her friend, but she knew that would just make matters worse. Instead, she decided to keep the news of Quadir to herself. She bent her head and began to cry. Her entire world was falling apart and there was nothing she could do to make it better.

Markita placed her hand on Gena's head and tried to comfort her friend.

"Come on, it's gonna be okay. Come on, I'll go with you to the hospital."

MONKEY SEE, MONKEY DO

Gena stood just outside the hospital door, afraid to open it, afraid to step inside, afraid to see her grandmother. She blamed herself for what happened to Gah Git. *If only I had been there, then maybe none of this would have happened. Oh, Gah Git, I'm so sorry.* Gena couldn't help but think that all this had something to do with Quadir's money. Since she had taken the money from Quadir's hidden apartment, her entire world had begun to go downhill. Nothing was right anymore. *I wish I had never found that apartment or that money.* Even though the attacker didn't ask for money, and only asked for her, it didn't matter. Gena had heard the saying "money is the root of all evil," and she was beginning to take the saying seriously. *What kind of monster would rape an old woman? Who is he? What does he want with me?* Nothing good, that's for sure. *He probably would have done the same to me or worse.* Gena started to think about everything that had happened. Like a bolt of lighting it hit her. *Quadir, oh, my God. He wants his money! He sent that guy to find me and look what he did.*

She reached down and felt her stomach. *Why would that guy do that to Gah Git?* She had so many unanswered questions; nothing made sense. But here she was today, standing outside a hospital room, scared to see her grandmother.

Gena slowly pushed open the door to the room and stepped inside. Gah Git was lying in bed with tubes protruding from various parts of her body. She was bandaged and bruised all over. Because of her age, the doctors were uncertain about the full extent of her recovery or if she would ever fully recover at all. As a result of being beaten and raped, Gah Git had required four separate surgeries to stop her internal bleeding. Gah Git's heart was sturdy—that was the good news. She had suffered several skull fractures from being struck with the handgun, and her bones were brittle because of her age. Healing was a coin toss. But they were going to do everything in their power to get the job done.

The doctors and the police had done the best they could to keep the incident out of the media, because an assault on an old woman would draw unbelievable media coverage, and perhaps cause even more deaths. These types of crimes often caused a chain reaction. Copycat killers sometimes come out of the woodwork on cases such as these. However, the efforts were worthless. The news spread through the city like wildfire. Other elderly people barricaded themselves indoors behind locks and chains, some refusing to go out even to get medical attention. Crimes like this reverberated across the community for months. And even though the detectives were upset about how the case was being handled in the media, they refused to comment. Their main reason was clear; they all had grandmothers and mothers, and something like this was inconceivable, inhuman even. A crime like this was done out of pure evil. Brutally beating and raping an old woman . . . no, they were going to lay this sick bastard to rest. When they caught him, his judge, his jury, and his sentence would be given to him inside a holding cell in a precinct house.

Gena approached her grandmother. She looked as though she had aged ten years since the last time Gena saw her. Gena bent down, kissed her forehead, and began to caress her arm softly, causing Gah Git to open her eyes.

She smiled at Gena.

"Hey, Gah Git," Gena said, barely audible. "How you feeling?"

Gah Git lifted an eyebrow, telling Gena how stupid her question was.

Tears fell from Gena's eyes. "Gah Git, I am so sorry! I don't know why someone would do something like this. I'm so, so, sorry. Please don't be mad at me."

Barely able to speak, Gah Git whispered, "I'm not mad at you," then reached up to wipe Gena's tears away. She placed her hand on top of Gena's gently, too weak to do much else. She looked into Gena's eyes and silently said everything would be okay without saying a word.

Gena wiped her tears and smiled and held Gah Git's hand. She leaned forward and buried her head in her grandmother's chest. Gah Git was so strong. *Only you Gah Git, only you.* Gena didn't know what it was but there was something about her grandmother that no matter what, she was able to see a bigger, better, brighter picture even when the world was dark and gray and hopeless. For Gena it seemed the older generation just had that way about them. No matter what, it was still okay and somehow the Lord would give whatever strength was needed. Maybe it was some damn magic potion that they drank when they were younger or something. Gena thought of all the stories her grandmother had told her about her mother and her father not being able to go to school and having to work the fields in the South, picking cotton all day in the hot sun. And she remembered Gah Git's stories of the sixties and seventies and the Black Panthers and the civil rights movement and Martin Luther King Jr., and Malcolm X. *Maybe that's why she's so much stronger than me.* Gena would never have thought of marching or boycotting, and would never have imagined Gah Git out there either. Yes, her grandmother, Gah Git, was one of the last few out there who endured the water hoses, the dogs, the police batons, the beatings, the jails, and everything else, and still she held up her head and kept going. Gena never understood how her grandmother managed to always take nothing and turn it into something. She would take in her grandbabies and accept the responsibility and all that came with them. She made sure they had food to eat and clean clothes on their backs. She helped each and every one of them with their school lessons and preached day in and day out about staying out of trouble. This was her Gah Git, and for Gena to know that she had caused her grandmother pain broke her heart in two.

Gah Git caressed Gena's head, and Gena could hear her grandmother trying to speak.

"Huh, Gah Git, what did you say?"

"Don't cry, baby," she whispered taking in small breaths.

Gena smiled at Gah Git and watched her close her eyes. She was on heavy sedation for the pain, and just like that like she was asleep.

"My life is so messed up right now and I have no one, Gah Git, no one. I don't know what to do and I don't know where

to begin. I'm pregnant, Gah Git. I'm going to have a baby."
She looked at her grandmother. Not even a flinch. Gah Git
was definitely sleeping. "I thought the guy that I was seeing
really cared about me. And when I went to tell him I was
pregnant, he tried to kill me. He was after Quadir's money and
he tried to kill me, but Quadir rescued me and then I found
out that all this time, Gah Git, he wasn't dead. Quadir didn't
die. He's been alive all this time. A doctor saved him and she
helped him recuperate. And he never came for me, he just let
me keep thinking he was dead and the guy I was seeing—oh,
Gah Git, it's such a mess—is the guy who tried to kill Quadir,
so Quadir hates me. He thinks I was in cahoots to bring him
harm. And I love him, Gah Git; I love him so much. It's just
that he doesn't love me anymore. He thinks I'm his enemy and
all he wants now is his money. And I'm starting to think that
it was Quadir who sent that man to the house looking for me
because I ran away. I snuck out the window and I left him.
But the only reason I left is because he told me about him and
the doctor. You should have heard the way he was talking, you
could tell that he really loves her. He doesn't love me no more,
Gah Git, and I wish he did. I wish he did."

Gena laid her head back down on her grandmother. Gah
Git had listened to every word Gena said. *Oh, Lord, what a
mess, Gena; what a mess you have made with your life.* Gah Git
wanted to speak so badly, but she didn't. She just lay still and
pretended to be asleep. She simply listened to what was going
on with her grandbaby. Truth was she knew if she opened her
eyes, Gena would stop talking. So, she lay there listening to
Gena talking about her sordid life.

When she was done spilling out her heart and soul Gena

walked out of the room and found Markita sitting among her family in the hospital's hallway.

Out of nowhere, like a sabertooth tiger, Gwendolyn jumped up and went over to Gena, who hadn't even had a chance to get the door closed.

"You lucky I don't fuck you up in here. See, see, see, all that shit with them gangster-ass niggas of yours got my mother all fucked up," said Gwendolyn, getting ready to swing at Gena.

"Fight, fight, fight," said Bria, who smacked high fives with her twin, Brianna, as they stood on the sidelines as if watching a Jerry Springer episode.

"Calm down; calm down," said Michael, grabbing his sister's arm and holding her back.

"No, Michael, let me go. She need her ass kicked. That little bitch wouldn't even help me get out of jail."

"Gah Git told me not to get you out," cried Gena. "And I don't know what's going on. Bria told me what happened. I swear I don't know who's looking for me."

"Well, take your ass on somewhere until you figure it out," said Gwendolyn.

"Stop, Gwendolyn. Just knock it off in this hospital making all this commotion," said Paula, who would rather see the family quarrel in the privacy of their home.

"Don't nobody want to hear that shit, Paula. Michael, let me go."

"You know what, Aunt Gwendolyn? You got so much to say about me, what about you? You broke Gah Git's heart, running around Richard Allen like a wild crack monkey. You really got some nerve," said Gena, ready to go toe to toe.

"Bitch, I'll whoop your little ass. Who you think you talking to. I'm your elder."

"Whatever, Aunt Gwendolyn. You're nothing but a crack monkey," said Gena as she was being pushed to the elevator by Paula and Bria while Michael and Gwendolyn's boyfriend, Royce, held Gwendolyn back.

"Come on, Gena. Just leave her alone; just come on," said Bria, pushing the buttons on the elevator panel and trying to close the door behind them.

"Aunt Gwendolyn is crazy, ain't she?" asked Bria.

"Yeah, she crazy all right. But, she's telling the truth, though."

"Gena, it's not your fault. You can't blame yourself or let nobody else put the blame on you. Regardless of whether or not some mad, crazed lunatic is looking for you, and raped our old-ass grandmother and done damn near killed Gar . . ."

"Bria, please, I get the point. It's just that, truth is, she's right."

"Well, what are you gonna do? 'Cause everybody is really scared for you, Gena. If that man would do that to Gah Git, Lord only knows what he'll do to you once he finds you."

She's right; there's no telling what he'll do. There's no telling what Quadir has told him to do. I better get out of town and quick. But where will I go?

"You okay? You look like you're just staring out into space."

"No, no, I'm fine. I'm okay."

"So, what you gonna do, Gena? You better get out of town while this crazy man is looking for you."

"Yeah, I know. I just can't believe he'd do something like this."

"Who?"

"Nobody, nothing," said Gena as she hugged her cousin.

"You gonna be okay?"

"Yeah, yeah, I'll be fine."

"Where you gonna go?"

"I don't know. I don't know."

It's probably better that you keep your whereabouts to yourself, especially since you got crazy rapists and murderers hunting you down, mmm-hmm, thought Bria as she watched the elevator doors close with her cousin on the other side of them.

MOMMIE DEAREST

Quadir strolled through the back door of his home, nearly scaring his mother to death.

"Quadir!" She rushed to him and embraced him tightly. "What are you doing here? You know you shouldn't be here! If someone sees you . . ."

"It's okay, Mama." Quadir nodded. "I just wanted to drop by and see you."

"Quadir, if you needed to see me, you could have just left the code, and I would have met you at the meeting place."

"I know. I just wanted to see you right now. I didn't feel like waiting."

Mrs. Richards exhaled. "Qua, boy, what's the matter?"

Quadir shook his head.

"This better not be about that damn money."

"Not really."

"Not really?" She placed her hands on her hips. "What does that mean?"

"It's about Gena."

Mrs. Richards turned back to her dirty dishes. "What about Gena?"

"She woke up."

Mrs. Richards froze. "And?"

"She knows it was me who rescued her."

She turned toward her son. "She knows you're alive?"

Quadir nodded.

"And so, what's next?"

Quadir shrugged. "That's the problem. I can't answer that question."

"Well, you know I can't answer it for you. So if it's those kinds of answers you're looking for, you've come to the wrong place. There's a mirror behind you. Turn around, and ask away, because that's the only person who can give you the answers you're looking for."

Quadir smiled. She was as blunt as always. And just as truthful. But like all of her truths, this one was also filled with many other truths. He had come here to find an answer, and he knew that she had the key to unlock the code that was keeping him from finding peace.

"Amelia says hi," Quadir said.

"Nice girl." Mrs. Richards faced her son. "I really like her. Nice, polite, honest, straightforward, smart. And a doctor, making her own money. What's not to like?" She turned back to her dishes and continued washing them.

Quadir nodded. "She does have everything going for her."

"Nice girl."

"You said that already."

"Did I?"

"You did."

"Hmm."

"Another hmm."

"Are you two getting serious?"

"I don't know."

"Why don't you know?"

"I don't know that either."

"Are you sure you don't know?" Viola asked with a knowing smile.

"A lot of loose ends to wrap up, I guess. I want to make sure one door is closed before I open up a new one."

"Wise to always do."

Quadir seated himself at the table and lowered his head to his arms.

"Sometimes doors are hard to close, son," she told him. "Sometimes, there's so much behind those doors that our heart won't let us close them."

"What if it has to be closed?"

"It's hard to say good-bye to the ones we love."

Quadir remained silent.

"You do love her, don't you?"

Quadir lifted his head and turned toward her.

"I mean, it takes a lot for someone, especially my son, to hang up his playboy hat, and actually settle down. She must have really been something special for you to have done that. I used to wonder what was so special about Gena that could make you do that."

Quadir remained silent.

"Do you remember, son?"

"Remember what?"

"What was so special about her that made you want to settle down and be with her?"

Quadir lowered his head. His mother had just sucker-punched him in his heart. He did remember. He remembered her smile, her innocence, that killer body. She was his G, and he was her Qua. She was from the projects. He was trying to make a dollar out of fifteen cents. He was balling, trying to shine so that they could have things that they never dreamed of having. He remembered the day he promised himself that he would always take care of her. He remembered when they went to the Bahamas and stayed over at the Valiant Hotel. He remembered the first time they made love on the beach. It was as if the drink was named just for them. He remembered everything about her. *Why did she have to fuck with Jerrell. Why?* Things would be so much easier if she hadn't fucked with him.

"Ah, so you do remember," Viola said. His silence and day-dreaming had answered her question.

"She met somebody else."

Mrs. Richards nodded. "She's young, the man she loved was murdered, and in her mind you were never coming back. I'm sure enough time passed by. I'm sure she mourned her loss and then moved on. Come on, what do you expect? You were dead, and you were never coming back." She turned to him. "I remember being met by those doctors in the hospital and being told that you were dead. I broke down right there and fell into that doctor's arms. The first thing I thought was, my poor baby. And then I thought about how I was never going to see you alive again, how I was never going to get to see that smile of yours, how I was never going to get to hold any grandchildren from you. My Quadir was dead, and he was never coming back. I was preparing for a funeral in my head, and preparing for a life without my baby. Right up until Amelia called and had me meet her in that damn parking garage across from the hospital. She snuck me into the intensive care unit late that night and allowed me to peek into your room. I got down on my knees and prayed so hard to God that night, thanking Him for giving me my baby back, that I couldn't walk for two days. I had the privilege of knowing that you were alive. I had the ability to sneak in and see you whenever I wanted. She didn't have those things. Your death to her was as sure as the sun sets in the evening time. She had to move on; she had to live."

"You don't understand, she was fucking with Jerrell, Mom. And he's the one who tried to kill me."

Viola finished her last dish and turned to her son. "It hurts like hell, and you feel betrayed by that. Quadir, I put that girl on the streets, so that I could hide the fact you were alive, and look for that damn money. Put her on the streets! That was the worst thing I have ever done in my entire life. She had nothing, and nowhere to go when I did that. We can't blame her for moving forward with life. She's strong, Quadir. She wasn't just going to curl up in a ball and die. I raised you to be a man. To stand up and be a man. No one is at fault here. You got shot, we had to protect you to keep you alive, she thought that you were dead, and life happened. It's life's fault. So, now you have a choice. You can go on and always wonder what if, or you can put those questions to rest."

"How?"

"Do you love her?"

Quadir went silent.

"Do you still love her?" Viola asked more forcefully.

"I love her."

"Then that's all that matters."

"And Amelia?"

"What about her?"

"I love her too."

"You love her for everything that she did for you? Or are you in love with her?"

Quadir shook his head. "That's just it; I don't know. She means everything to me. She's everything that I've never had in a woman. She's independent, she's smart, she's fun to be around, she's strong. She puts my ass in check when I need it. I've never met anybody like her."

"Well, that's because she's independent and not no project chickenhead, like you're used to."

Quadir laughed. "Mom!"

"You dating these hoochies looking for some tennis shoes and something to eat, and maybe get an outfit and their hair and nails done. Let's keep it real." She kissed Quadir on top of his head. "And for the first time in my baby's life, he's met a real black woman. A strong sister, who tells him to keep his money in his pocket; she's got this. She doesn't need anything from you, Quadir. She just wants your love."

"And I want to give it to her. She deserves it."

"Don't give it to her because you think you owe it to her, baby. One thing about women like Amelia, they always land on their feet. No matter what decision you make, even if your decision is to make none at all, she's going to be all right."

Quadir exhaled. "You got a quarter?"

"A quarter? What for?"

"Hell, for the coin toss. I don't know what the hell I'm gonna do."

Viola threw her head back in laughter. Quadir joined in.

"Follow your heart, Quadir."

"My heart is pulling me in two different directions."

She shook solemnly. "No it's not. It's pulling you in one direction, but your pride and sense of duty are pulling you in another. You don't owe anyone anything. You don't owe Amelia anything for saving your life. She's a doctor; it's her job. You don't owe those niggas on the street no explanation. You don't owe Gena and who cares what she did in the midst of your absence? Listen, son, you make your decisions in life based on what will make you happy. You were given a second chance to live. Take it. Don't let nothing stop you from living your life to the fullest and being happy."

Quadir nodded. "I thought you liked Amelia better."

"I do. What mother wouldn't want their child to marry a doctor? But hell, I'm from the hood so I'll always root for the underdog. Listen, it's not that I don't like Gena or that I like Amelia better; you're the one that gots to lay up with the broad. Shoot, not me. I just want you to make whatever decision will make you happy. I'm your mother; I love you—that's what mothers do."

SNEAKY SNEAKY

Rik pulled up to the shopping center in his black Range Rover and found a parking space up front. Today was a good day for shopping. He had a little change left over, and he might as well get some new kicks. Even if he wasn't balling out of control like before, there was no sense in looking like shit. He lived by the mantra "never let 'em see you sweat." So even though times were desperate, he was still going to look as if he were the fucking king of Philly.

The clothing store that he chose today was one of his favorites. It was a small Italian clothier that sold fine Italian suits. They could hand-make you a suit, or tailor something off the rack to fit you just right. They also carried the latest in street gear in another section of the store. Today, he was here to do a little bit of shopping for both.

Rik stepped into the shop and waved to the owner's son, Anthony. Anthony was a typical young Italian. He wore the flyest tailored suits out there, but fucked them up by wearing too much jewelry. He had a Rolex on one wrist, a Rolex bracelet on the other, three rings on his left-hand fingers, and four rings on his right-hand fingers . . . way too much.

Rik headed for the suits. He was going to find something on the rack and have it tailored to his specifications. Charcoal was the color he needed, something in a really dark gray color, not too close to black, but none of that light gray shit either. Something that looked fly. He already had the shoes and a tie that would go perfectly with what he had in mind.

"Well hello, Tyrik!" Detective Ellington greeted him from behind.

"Spending a little bit of that dope money today, are we?" Detective Davis asked, stepping to the other side of Rik.

Rik saw that the detectives had him boxed in. "Man, what y'all want?"

"We're putting together a greatest-hits mix tape," Ellington told him. "We got your soundtrack from the dope deals you made."

"And your conversations with your cellmate while you were in jail," Davis added.

"And of course the best one of all, your conversation with Ms. Scott," Ellington told him.

"You know, the one where she offered you the money to make a two-million-dollar bond," Davis added, placing his arm around Rik.

Instantly Rik became nervous. *How the fuck do they know that?*

"I don't know what y'all are talking about," Rik told them.

"Ah, ah, ah, ah. Let's not play stupid, Tyrik," Davis said. "Don't make me pull out my little tape recorder and play it back for you."

Ellington shook her head and whispered into Rik's ear. "You

really don't want him to pull out the tape recorder. It really pisses him off when he has to do that. Besides, if we listen to all those tapes of you discussing drug deals and drug money, we might find reason to indict you once again."

"Okay." Rik lifted his hands in surrender. "What do you want from me?"

"The offer your little friend made to you . . . do you think that you can get her to make it again?" Ellington asked.

"What, the offer to post my bond?" Rik asked. "Why would she do that? I'm not in jail."

Davis produced a pair of handcuffs. "That's not a problem. I can definitely make that happen."

"I haven't done shit!" Rik protested.

"You think that means something to me?" Davis asked with a crooked smile.

"Let's just say, we have an arrangement to make with you," Ellington told him.

"And that would be?" Rik asked, lifting an eyebrow.

"We want you to borrow some money from her," Ellington told him.

"For what?"

"To keep your black ass out of prison!" Ellington snapped. "However much you want, just so long as it's an emergency, and she'll loan it to you. She offered it to you once, right?"

"What, you want to get her on tape offering me some money?" Rik asked. "I ain't wearing no wire!"

"No, dipshit, we already have her on tape offering you the money!" Davis told him. "Can you get her to loan you the money or what?"

"Maybe," Rik said, looking at the pair of oink-oinks standing in front of him. "What's in it for me?"

Davis and Ellington exchanged glances. "Um, like besides staying out of jail, you get to keep whatever you can get her to loan you," Ellington replied.

"Bullshit!" Rik said, looking at Letoya as if she were out of her mind. "This is a setup."

Davis shoved Rik up against a clothing rack. "This ain't no bullshit, boy! You either cooperate with us, or we'll make your life a living hell. You got that?"

Rik nodded.

"Good." Ellington stuffed one of her cards into Rik's pocket. "If she agrees, you contact me ASAP. You got that?"

Rik nodded.

Ellington and Davis turned and exited the store. Davis turned to his partner. "There ain't no way in hell we're letting him keep that money."

Ellington nodded. "I know, but it sounded good, right?"

Davis laughed and climbed into the car.

Inside, Rik straightened out his clothing. *What the fuck is wrong with the police? Those two must be out their minds. If they think for one second that they're getting in on my meal ticket, they can forget it.* There was no way he was calling them, or doing anything else for them or with them. He pulled the detective's card from his pocket, tore it up, and tossed it over his shoulder. He was here to enjoy himself, relax, and shop, and that was exactly what he planned to do.

The Clam Bar and Pat's Cheese Steaks in South Philly was where everyone hung out on the weekend, especially after the clubs closed down at two in the morning. Grabbing something to eat and hanging out on the smaller streets of South Philly was a longstanding Saturday night ritual for Philly's young hip-hop partygoers. Showing off their new clothes or skimpy outfits and their souped-up cars with shiny rims was the thing to do.

And if you were a female, being with a hot boy was also the thing to do. Kevvy Kev's 5.0 Mustang Convertible GT made him a hot boy, and that was one of the reasons Bria made him her boyfriend. Kevvy Kev's 5.0 was burgundy, with a ground-effects kit and a massive whale tail in the back. It was sitting on seventeen-inch all-gold Daytons that matched the car's peanut-butter interior and gold trim. And Kevvy Kev's stereo system was off the chain as well. Without a doubt, Kevvy Kev had the cleanest ride on the scene every weekend. Bria loved to be seen inside that car, especially when the top was down and the system was booming. They would joyride for hours, riding around the city aimlessly.

Tonight Kevvy Kev had the top down, and everybody was out and about. The weather had finally cleared, and for the first time in a long time the stars were visible.

"What do you want outta here?" Kevvy Kev asked.

"Get me a cheese steak with fried onions, mayonnaise, ketchup, and salt and pepper. And get some cheese fries and a Pepsi," Bria told him.

Kevvy Kev climbed out of the car, and Bria caressed his behind. She loved herself some Kevvy Kev. And so did a lot of other girls, she knew. She had already gotten into four fights over him, but that was okay, because to her he was worth fighting for. Kevvy Kev had the most dreamy brownish-green eyes that a girl could ever imagine. She loved it when he sat between her legs while she cornrolled his long hair, and he would stare up at her with those damn emeralds he called eyes. And those lips of his were the sexiest lips she had ever come across.

She loved to suck on them; they felt like orange slices in her mouth. She was getting wet just thinking about how fine and how cute he was.

"Hey, Bria!"

She turned to see who was calling to her. A car filled with football players from her high school pulled into the parking lot next to her.

"What's up, baby?" one of them, a guy named Troy, asked her. "When you gonna drop that half-breed zero and get with this hero?"

"When that hero gets his own car and stops riding in the backseat of somebody else's."

"Oh, it's like that, huh?" Troy asked.

"Troy, you not even riding shotgun yet; you still backseat, right passenger side window."

The rest of the guys in the car started clowning Troy.

"Bria, you know you fine as hell," the driver told her.

"Marcus, don't even start, 'cause you know me and Stephanie is friends. And you know I'll tell her everything that you say to me."

"Girl, why you tripping?" Marcus asked.

"Where is Brianna's fine ass at?" J-Roc asked.

Bria shrugged. "I don't know; what I look like, her keeper or something?"

"Here come your busted-ass nigga!" Troy told her. "You need to come and get some of this pure black Mandingo, and leave those Vienna sausages alone!"

The boys cranked up their car and pulled away laughing. Kevvy Kev returned and passed Bria her food.

"What the hell they talking about?" he asked.

Bria shrugged. "Nothing, as usual."

Kevvy Kev climbed into his car and closed the door. Bria opened up her food and began eating.

"Bria, right?"

Bria peered up from her sandwich. She had never seen his face before. And he was way too old to be in high school. "Do I know you?"

"No, but you know the person I'm looking for," Terrell told her.

"Do I look like the Yellow Pages to you?" Bria asked, craning her neck.

"Cute." Terrell smiled. "Real cute." He pulled out the picture of Gena and held it up. "Where's your cousin?"

Bria's eyes flew wide. Instantly, she knew that this was the man who had hurt her grandmother. "I don't know where she is!"

"Say, man! Go on with all of that bullshit!" Kevvy Kev said forcefully. "Can't you see we eating?"

"I wasn't talking to you," Terrell told him.

"Yeah, well I was talking to you!" Kevvy Kev opened his door and started to climb out of the car.

Terrell pulled out a handgun and shot Kevvy Kev in the groin. The sound of gunfire caused pandemonium, and people began to flee.

Terrell grabbed a screaming Bria by her hair and pulled her face closer to Gena's picture. "Where is she?"

"I don't know!" Bria shouted. "I haven't seen her but once since she moved out!"

"Where did she move to?"

"I don't know! I think she moved in with her friend!"

"What friend? Give me a name."

"Markita!" Bria shouted. "Her friend Markita!"

Terrell let go of her hair. "Are you lying to me?" He pointed his weapon at a squirming, crying Kevvy Kev.

Bria leaned over and shielded her man from the gun. "No! I'm not lying! She moved in with her friend!"

Terrell nodded and tucked his gun away. He could hear the faint sound of sirens in the distance. "If you're lying to me, I'll find you, and next time, it'll be you that I bend over and fuck like there's no tomorrow. You understand me?"

Bria nodded, scared as all back doors as she looked into the eyes of a madman.

Terrell leaned over and stuck his tongue into her mouth for several seconds before rushing to his car and peeling away.

Gena rose to her feet and looked around the hotel suite she had been staying in now for the past several weeks. After her visit to the hospital to see Gah Git, Gena had decided it was best not to go anywhere near her family or anyone else she cared about. She walked into the bathroom and turned on the sink faucet. She looked at herself in the mirror. *Today is the big day, no turning back,* she thought as she splashed some water across her face and reached for a washrag.

Gena showered and dressed, packed up a small carry-on, and left the room. A continental breakfast was being served in the hotel's lobby, but Gena would have to pass on that. *I wish I could just have something to drink. My mouth is so dry,* she thought, knowing that food and water were out of the question. Gena made her way out to the parking lot where she had parked the Mazda rental. She got into the car, exited the lot, and drove over to Thirty-eighth and Lancaster. Across the street from a bar was a women's health clinic. She looked at her watch. It was 8:42 in the morning, her appointment was scheduled for nine. *Are you ready?* She couldn't help but ask herself this question. Her mind roamed constantly as she parked the car and walked into the clinic.

"Hi. Your name?" asked the receptionist behind the counter.

"Gena Scott. I have a nine-o'clock appointment," Gena said.

"Okay, here you go; have a seat and fill these papers out. Make sure you sign the bottom of each form where indicated."

After Gena completed the forms and gave them back to the receptionist, she went back to her seat. Minutes later her name was called and she followed a woman to the second floor of the clinic.

"Have you eaten or had anything to drink since midnight last night?" the woman asked.

"No," Gena responded.

She put Gena in an examining room, and took her weight, blood pressure, and temperature. She asked her one hundred and one questions and finally told her to undress and put on a hospital gown. She said the doctor would be in shortly and then she left the room.

Gena lay on the table and rubbed her belly. She thought of having a baby, and the thought alone scared her half to death. Then she thought of her grandmother. Gah Git would cry a hundred and one tears if she knew Gena was having an abortion. She thought of Jerrell and the times that they did have sex, how gentle and loving he was. She thought of the night he tried to kill her and realized she had been tricked by a horrible monster. Then she thought of Quadir. *I know if I have Jerrell's baby, there's no chance, no chance at all, that he'll ever be with me again. He'd only hate me even more.* No, Gena knew that if she had a baby by Jerrell Jackson, she could kiss Quadir Richards good-bye. *He's mad enough at the fact that I was messing with Jerrell—to have his baby, no way.* No, Gena knew she was doing the right thing. She just wished that it was over.

Dr. Amerson entered the room and sat down at the end of the table that Gena was lying on. Quickly, she went through a series of questions—basically the same questions she had already answered. Then she asked her if was she ready.

"Yes, yes, I am."

Dr. Amerson explained the procedure and attempted to make her feel comfortable with the knowledge of what would be happening. Once the procedure was complete, she would be moved into a room and placed on a recliner, where she would have to stay for at least two hours before she would be permitted to leave. The anesthetic would make her drowsy, and the rule was that she would have to call a cab to come and get her. Her intention was to have the cab take her around the block and right back across the street to her car. She knew to be careful driving, but she wasn't going far. Her plan was to have the abortion and then go check into the Sheraton Hotel on Thirty-eighth and Chestnut, just a few blocks away. She could definitely make it there.

A nurse entered the room with a needle and small bottle. Dr. Amerson explained that they were going to mildly sedate her. She wouldn't be asleep during the procedure, but she wouldn't feel a thing. Gena turned her head away, not wanting to watch as the nurse injected the anesthetic into her bloodstream.

Gena began to feel light, as if lying on a cloud. She looked around the room and it was as if an angel appeared right in front of her.

"Sahirah?"

And just like that the angel was gone.

"Okay, I'm going to lift your feet and place them in the stirrups. I'm going to insert my fingers; okay, Gena. I just want to examine your uterus before we get started." She could hear Dr. Amerson's voice.

"Dr. Amerson, I don't know. I don't know if I should go through with it."

"Gena, just give me one minute."

"Is everything okay?"

"Well, everything seems to be okay, but . . . Nurse, please hand me her chart and prep the sonogram machine."

"What, what's the matter?" said Gena in a state of semiconsciousness.

"Gena, your uterus feels normal. Just let me finish examining you, okay? Now, let me see, you were here three weeks ago, right? Yes, and you were six weeks pregnant. Let me count and make sure, yes, you were here and you were definitely pregnant." Dr. Amerson turned on the monitor of the sonogram machine, only to find that Gena's uterus was intact. She wasn't pregnant.

"Gena, I'm so sorry. You've obviously suffered a miscarriage."

Gena heard what Dr. Amerson said and the strangest feeling of relief came over her. She didn't feel sad. She had no remorse. Actually, she was ready to celebrate. All she could think about was the possibility of winning Quadir back.

Using all her strength, she snatched her foot out of the doctor's hand. Gena tried to lift herself up, but was too groggy.

"Here, here, it's okay. I got you," said Dr. Amerson, helping her off the table. "Let's see if we can't get you into recovery and you can wait there for the anesthetic to wear off."

"Do you believe this? Isn't this the most wonderful news?" She started crying. "You just don't know what this means for me."

This was probably the only thing Gena knew for sure. Maybe, just maybe anyone else's, but Jerrell's child, for Quadir to have to look after, was the last thing on this earth that would ever have happened, and Gena knew it.

"It means you don't have to have an abortion," answered the nurse. "Come on, we have crackers and juice. I know you're hungry. Come on, hold on to me and I'll get you situated."

Gena held on to the nurse and followed her into recovery. She lay on a recliner and was given a blanket. Within minutes Gena nodded off to sleep.

WIRES

Dick Davis rushed through the halls of the police department like a schoolboy who had just received his first kiss. His smile was uncontrollable, and he pushed aside police officer after police officer, making his way back to his partner's desk. His excitement was electric.

"What?" Detective Ellington asked, peering up from her desk. Her partner's smile made her smile. It was infectious.

Davis held up a cassette tape. "Hot off the presses! I just came from the recording room. Guess what our wiretaps just intercepted?"

"What?"

"She's leaving!" Davis told her giddily. "She blowing town! Which means?"

"She's got to get the money." Ellington stood and grabbed her purse. "How soon do you think she's leaving?"

"Who knows. You figure she's probably got to tie up a few loose ends, but trust me, she won't leave that money behind. If she's got it, then it will be going with her."

"Call Cornell and fill him in," Ellington told him. "Do we have anybody tailing her right now?"

Davis shook his head, "Nah, not that I know of."

"We need someone on her twenty-four-seven from now on." Ellington threw her purse onto her shoulder. "I'm going to see Mark and let him know."

"You want me to have narcotics put a tail on her?"

Ellington shook her head. "Those guys are idiots. They all think they're on *Miami Vice* or something. She'll spot them a million miles away. We'll all just have to take turns tailing her."

Davis nodded and lifted the telephone. Ellington strutted down the hall to see her boss, Lieutenant Mark Ratzinger.

"In!" Ratzinger shouted.

Ellington strutted into his office and plopped down in the chair opposite his desk.

"What's up, Toya?"

"We got her."

Ratzinger lifted his head from his paperwork.

"Her? As in her?"

Ellington nodded. "Ms. Money Bags. She's trying to skip town."

Ratzinger lifted his telephone without saying another word to Ellington. "Hey, Sammy, this is Mark over in vice. I need you to put a tail on a suspect for me." Ratzinger lifted a paper from his desk. "Gena Scott. License plate Sierra, Charlie, Alpha, six, five, six. Keep the tail loose; this is a priority suspect. And if you can, give me details of all her stops. Thanks, Sammy."

"You really want those guys in on this?" Ellington asked.

Ratzinger shrugged. "They're just going to follow her. Every

time she stops, they'll call me, and I'll call you. Get out in the
streets and be ready for my call."

Ellington nodded.

"Anybody call Cleaver yet?"

"Dickie's doing it now."

Ratzinger shook his head. "I don't trust that guy. I know
he's your ex-partner, but it's something about him . . ."

Ellington nodded. "He is one to be watched closely."

"I want this one controlled. No coming back on us."

Ellington nodded.

"I want you to handle it. Handle everything, you understand?" Ratzinger asked, wondering if Ellington had gotten
his point.

"I'll put a hole in the little cunt's forehead myself."

Ratzinger nodded. "Good." *She got my point*, he thought.

Ellington rose and hurried out of the room.

Ratzinger sipped from his cup of warm coffee, then rubbed
his tired eyes. He couldn't believe that things were finally coming together. He shifted through the papers on his desk until
he found his boating magazine. He turned to the classified
pages in the back and stared at the boat he had been dreaming
about since the current issue came out. He could see himself retired, sailing off the shores of Cape Cod in the four-
hundred-thousand-dollar beauty. He was one or two days
away from having the money to leave this shit behind, one or
two days away from having the money for his dream boat. He
couldn't wait.

Ellington stormed out of the police station and climbed into
her car. Davis was right on her heels. As soon as he hopped
inside, they were on their way. Neither paid any attention

to the gray van parked in the corner of the police station parking lot.

"I can't believe you!" Agent Phil Covington shouted, tossing his headset onto the console. "We're dead! We are so dead! Galvani is going to fire us, and then kill us!"

"He's not going to fire us," Agent Josh Harbinger replied. "Lavon, tell him."

"He's not going to fire you," Agent Lavon Stokes said flatly, without peering up from her computer.

"Yeah, right! He's going to fire us all, and then he's going to shoot us, and then he's going to throw us in jail!"

"He's not going to throw us in jail," Josh told him with a smile.

"He didn't authorize this! There's no way you can get me to believe that Galvani authorized this!" Phil said hysterically.

"Authorized what?" Josh smiled.

"Josh! You bugged a police station! Jesus! You bugged a lieutenant's office! A lieutenant who just happens to be in charge of the vice squad!"

"A dirty lieutenant, I remind you." Josh retorted.

"We wouldn't have known that unless we bugged him!" Phil threw himself back in his chair. "Josh, we are in so much trouble. We have broken so many statutes that it isn't funny! And you brought me along! How could you have done this to me!"

Josh patted Phil on the shoulder. "Relax, Phil. You're going to be a hero. Tell him, Lavon."

"You're going to be a hero," Lavon said flatly, without peering up from her computer.

"See, Lavon sees the big picture," Josh told him. "We've got them on conspiracy to commit extortion, murder, robbery, and about a half dozen other criminal statutes."

"Oh, God, what am I going to tell my mother when I get fired?" Phil lamented.

"You're not getting fired," Josh told him, then he added, "Lavon."

"You're not getting fired," she said just as flatly as she had before, still focused on the screen of her computer.

"Do you think they get care packages in Terre Haute federal prison?" Phil asked.

"Yes, but you're not going to Terre Haute," Josh told him. "We're sending those assholes to federal prison. We need backup. Lavon, you got that license plate number?"

"Sure did."

"Call Rich and tell him to tail her. No, change that. Tell him to tail them. We want to catch them when they're making their move. If they see a tail on her, they may back off. Let him know that it's cops he's tailing, so hang back and be on his Ps and Qs."

"I can't believe you bugged the police department," Phil whined.

"Phil, we're going to save this girl and put away a bunch of crooked cops. See, I told you that bastard Cleaver was dirty!"

Lavon nodded. "You did say that."

"Did you at least get a judge to sign off on the wiretaps?" Phil asked.

Josh smiled deviously, looking like Brad Pitt's twin. "I did."

Phil shook his head. "No, no you didn't. Josh, please tell me you didn't."

Josh nodded. "I did."

"You got my father to sign off on the warrant?" Phil asked incredulously.

Josh nodded and smiled. "I did. Your father is a federal magistrate."

"This whole thing is bordering on illegal. Christ, I'm going to spend the rest of my life in a federal penitentiary," Phil whined.

"Improper, not illegal," Josh corrected. "Lavon, we need to get this tape in front of a grand jury pronto. Who's the best deputy United States district attorney to get this to?"

"Watts, I'd say, seeing as how this thing was so fast and loose."

"Can you get this over to Watts for me?"

Lavon exhaled. "Why did I know you were going to say that?"

Josh kissed her on her cheek. "I got to go and smooth things out with Galvani. Get him on board."

Phil shook his head. "Galvani's going to kill you."

"We're heroes, Phil. Relax."

"What am I supposed to do in the meantime?"

"Check with the guys in the van over at Philly PD's headquarters."

"Another van? You got another van? You brought more guys in on this thing? Who'd you bug over there, the chief of police?"

Josh smiled. "Cleaver's office."

"You bugged Internal Affairs?" Phil exhaled. "We're dead."

"We're FBI agents, and we're going to put those crooked sons-a-bitches away for good!" Josh reassured him. He fixed his collar and climbed out of the surveillance van. "Phil."

"What?"

"Smile."

HOLD ME DOWN

Hello?"

"Hey, Gena, this is Rik. What's up?"

"Hey, Rik! How ya doing?"

"Trying to make it, but it's hard, lil' mamma."

"Shit, you telling me. My whole life has been turned upside down this last month. Really, since Qua . . ."

"I know. I miss that nigga too. You know, Qua was my boy."

Silence fell for several moments as Gena thought of yesteryears and Rik thought of what to say next.

"Hey, Gena. I need to talk to you about something."

"What's up?"

"When I was locked up, you offered to hook your boy up with a little something-something."

"Yeah . . ."

"When I got knocked, they found everything. And everything wasn't mine. I owed some people. And the people I owed aren't a very understanding bunch. They came to see me, and they let me know what was going to happen if they didn't get they bread."

"Damn. I'm sorry to hear that. Rik, you know I'm here for you."

"I was hoping that you would say that. I need to get these guys off of my back, and then come up. You know me, Gena, it won't take long for me to get back on my feet."

"I know you a hustler, boy."

"Can you do me something?"

"What you talking?"

"A half a ticket, no more. I can get it all back to you in a couple months. Say four months at the latest."

"That's a lot of bread, Rik. Besides, I wasn't planning on being around here four months from now."

Damn, bitch, a month ago you had two mil to get me out of jail, now a half is a problem? Rik couldn't help his greed, but he didn't want it to show. "Gena, this is your boy. I'm good for it. And even if you ain't around here, planes fly. I'll take it to wherever you at."

"Damn, why now?" *How the hell am I going to get the money and get it to him, and do everything else I need to do before I fly the chicken coop?*

"Gena, you're the only person I can turn to. They gonna kill me, and my whole family, if I don't pay them."

"All right. I'll get it to you. But you gonna have to meet me today."

"No, problem; just tell me when and where."

"Um, let me think." Gena thought of all she had to do and the places she had to go. "Okay, I'll call you when I'm ready."

"Cool. Thanks, baby."

"Talk to you later."

"Bye."

"Later."

Quadir strolled across the lanai and seated himself on a recliner near the pool. The maid had set him a tall glass of ice-
cold lemonade out by the pool, and he wanted to take in the
sunset and relax. He had a lot on his mind, a lot of things that
he had to make sense of.

He couldn't help replaying his last conversation with Gena
before she snuck out to only God knew where. In a way, it
was his fault. Maybe if he had stopped her when he first had
the chance at the apartment building that night, she would
never have gotten onto the highway, never have stopped at
that gas station, and never have met Jerrell. *Damn, he was really going to kill her.* She had gotten caught up in something
that was completely beyond her control. He thought back to
New Year's Eve and the night he was gunned down, the night
he almost died. He remembered how scared she looked, how
broken she was, how her tears and screams for him flew freely
out of her. He could hear her voice begging him not to leave
her, begging him to hold on, begging him not to die. She
hadn't asked for him to be shot, and she hadn't asked for him
to die before her eyes. It wasn't her fault that she was forced
out onto the street, forced to survive without him, without
anything, and forced to make something out of nothing. She
was just playing the cards she was dealt. And now, it seemed as
if she had been dealt the losing hand.

"Hey, you okay? You always seem like you're miles away,"
said Amelia as she bent and kissed Quadir on the side of his
face.

"Yeah, I'm fine. What are you doing here? Aren't you suppose to be at the hospital?"

"Would you believe I have the afternoon off? I know, go figure. There was a mixup with the schedules. So I have an entire day to play house with you," she said, unable to control her smile as she sat on his lap, straddling him like a pony.

"Wow," said Quadir, never once taking his mind off Gena's situation. He pulled Amelia closer to him and kissed her lips.

"Oh, and did you hear what happened?"

"No, what?"

"Haven't you heard the news?"

"Yeah?"

"I overheard my colleagues talking about an elderly woman who had been beaten and raped. She underwent surgery and was placed in ICU. They asked me to look at her chart and check on her. Which I did. I looked in on her, and it turned out the elderly woman is Gena's grandmother."

"Really?" Quadir gave her his full attention. He had had absolutely no idea that the family on the news was Gena's.

Amelia shrugged. "She suffered some pretty traumatic injuries. She's having a lot of complications."

"What type of injuries?"

Amelia shook her head and looked down. "She was raped, Quadir, brutally raped and brutally beaten. She has all kinds of injuries, from internal bleeding to a concussion."

"I didn't hear all that on the news. She was raped?"

"Yes, and beaten."

"Damn, I can't believe it," he said as he began to pace up and down the lanai.

"I thought you heard the news."

"Yeah, but I wasn't paying attention, you know?"

How can you pay attention to anything when all you do is daydream about Gena and your hidden treasure?

"Do the police know anything? Did they get the bastard who did it?"

Amelia shook her head. "No suspects, from what I hear."

"Raped. That's crazy, right?"

"Sick, really sick," Amelia agreed.

Quadir shook his head. "She's an old woman. Who in the fuck would do that to an old woman?"

"A sick and crazy man," Amelia whispered. "There was also the grandson, Gary Scott. He's the one that tried to protect her, but the rapist shot him in the stomach. So I checked in on him also."

"How's he doing?"

"He'll live, but he's going to need multiple surgeries. He was shot in the stomach, you know, his lower intestine is useless for now. He'll probably wear a bag for the rest of his life unless surgery can correct it."

"A shit bag?"

"Um, yeah, if that's what you want to call it. Then there's another granddaughter, Bria Scott, who was assaulted by this same guy. The police brought the girl into the ER. I saw her, but I didn't treat her."

"Well, what happened?"

"Apparently this rapist guy felt her up and kissed her on the mouth after shooting her date, who was also brought into the ER, but died on the operating table. I think his name was Kevin Coffield. Police had the medics swab the girlfriend's tongue for DNA at the crime scene. I guess they checked it against the DNA taken from the grandmother and got a match."

"Damn, that's crazy," said Quadir, thinking things over. "No wonder I can't find Gena. I bet she's scared to death."

"Yeah, she probably thinks it's you coming after your money. I'm sure she's avoiding you like the plague."

"Why would you say something like that?" Quadir asked, taking offense.

"Gosh, I'm just saying, she was here, realized you were alive, and not only have you moved on, but you want your money back. She leaves, out the window, and never returns. She's not come back and she's not made any contact. She knows she has your money; she knows that you want it, I'm sure. Meanwhile, someone attacks her grandmother and her cousins, allegedly looking for her. In her mind, who else would be looking for her, except you, for your money? Which technically is correct because that's exactly what you do every day with your life."

"So, it's not random?" asked Quadir, completely ignoring her sarcasm.

Amelia shook her head. "Some fucking animal is fucking with them." Amelia nodded solemnly. "And he's after Gena."

"Maybe he's not after Gena, maybe you just think that," said Quadir, really hoping Amelia didn't know what she was talking about.

"Well, after I heard my colleagues talking about the family of patients they had treated, I spoke to a friend of mine who is a detective at the Thirty-first Precinct. She told me that in both incidents, the rapist was looking for Gena."

"Somebody's after Gena? What the fuck for?"

Amelia lifted an eyebrow as if stating the obvious. Quadir nodded, once his mind caught up.

"They want my money!"

"Bingo!"

"Jesus, that fucking money! Talk about more money more problems. Somebody's after my money!"

"Your money and God only knows what else," Amelia said as she rubbed Quadir's arm. "She's in danger," said Amelia as she rose and lifted her shirt over the top of her head to reveal a stunning two-piece.

"And the police are probably trailing her ass four cars deep trying to catch this guy."

"They don't know where she is, Qua. She's disappeared, gone underground."

Quadir leaned back on the sofa. His mind was trying to process all of the information.

"The police can't find her, but I bet if there's one person who could find her, it's you," Amelia said softly before kissing his cheek, then jumping into the swimming pool for a couple of laps.

I can't believe someone hurt her grandmother. That's some sick shit. Not only was her grandmother attacked, but her cousin, Gary, had also been shot, not to mention the attack on Bria's boyfriend, and the police said they were all related. They didn't release the motive and claimed they had no clues as to who the assailant was. Quadir remembered that the reporter also indicated that the family had refused to cooperate with the police, giving them very little information to go on. There was a lot going on, too much going on. *I wonder if Gah Git is going to be okay.* Quadir knew how much Gena loved her grandmother. Gah Git was all that Gena had for most of her life. Their recent conversation had been a good one at first; he had learned so much about what she felt, about what she went through. She still loved him and that gave him an added comfort despite the fact that they weren't together.

"Why are you still sitting here? It's getting dark, you know." Amelia emerged from the pool. She tied a towel around her narrow waist and ventured toward him. Quadir watched her the entire way.

Amelia's body was banging. She had the perfect frame, the perfect ass, the perfect size breasts and perfectly sized legs, but her feet were the most beautiful feet Quadir had ever seen in his life. Amelia was toned and firm, the product of a dedicated diet-and-exercise routine. Not to mention she was beautiful, even more so than Gena, and Gena had been his dream. Amelia had the most beautiful face he had ever seen, along with a head full of brains. She was a winner in anybody's book, a twenty, on a scale of one to ten. And yet, he found himself torn between his feelings for her and his feelings for Gena.

"What's the matter?" Amelia asked, sliding onto the lounge chair with him.

Quadir shook his head. "You know what's the matter."

"Money, police, Gena, crazy rapists on the loose. What else?"

What else is there? he couldn't help thinking but didn't say a word.

Amelia rose from the chaise. "My offer still stands, Qua. You can forget about the money. We can take my money, and I'll move with you wherever you want me to. You can go back to school, you can open a business, you can do whatever the fuck you want to."

"I just have to love you."

"That's all I'll ever ask. Just love me, baby. I don't need anything else."

That's it, just leave the money, leave everything, and go with Amelia. The offer was tempting, and it wasn't the first time that Amelia had thrown it out there. But Quadir couldn't accept it. He couldn't accept abandoning his fortune, with the thought of Gena having his money for God knows who to spend it. It just didn't sit right with him. Fair was fair, and while she might have found it, he hadn't given it to her. She took it. And he was determined to get it back.

Amelia turned to leave him reveling in his money schemes and thoughts of Gena, but Quadir wouldn't let her get away that easily. He yanked the towel from around her waist and examined her voluptuous curves. The sight of her slim waist, full hips, and perfectly round ass gave him an instant erection. He quickly leaped up from the recliner and clasped her wrist.

"You don't need nothing else?" Quadir gestured, pulling her close to him so she could feel the bulge in his shorts.

"Well, I do need one more thing, daddy . . . please," Amelia said in a sexy, whispering, moaning sort of way as she leaned in to his ear. Amelia shoved Quadir back down onto the lounge chair and yanked his shorts down to his ankles. "Hmm. Somebody is really excited."

Quadir grabbed his meat and stroked it a few times.

"Gimme that," she said as she moved her string bikini to the side and climbed on top of him. *I bet you ain't thinking about her now.* Quadir wanted to explode as soon as he felt her insides wrap around his dick, pulling at it with each stroke. He leaned back, gripped her ass, spread her cheeks apart, and held on for the ride.

BIG PIMPIN'

Gena had planned her day very carefully. It took much planning, and a little help from her family, to make things work. She just hoped that Brianna had planted the car in the right spot, and that Bria had handled her part. If they had, then things would go smoothly, or at least that's what she was praying for.

Gena parked her car and strolled into the mall hoping that whoever her pursuers were, they would see her and wait in the parking lot for her to come out. Her plan depended on it.

Gena rushed through the shopping mall and into the department store where Bria worked. She made her way through the store to the junior miss department, which was her cousin's department. Gena spied Bria behind the counter helping a customer. She made eye contact, and then stopped and pretended to be browsing through some dresses. Gena tried her damndest, but couldn't tell one way or the other if she had been followed into the Gallery or not.

Bria finished up with her customer, then grabbed a dress

and some shoes that she had held behind the counter. She also grabbed a large straw sun hat, a large handbag, and some sunglasses, and headed for the women's changing area. Gena continued to browse through the department's offerings until Bria returned to her counter and gave her a nod. Gena turned and headed for the dressing area.

Inside the dressing area, Gena walked from stall to stall, opening each door until she found the clothing that Bria had left for her. Once she found the right stall, she stepped inside, locked the door, and changed clothes.

The clothing change took less than four minutes. She turned and examined herself in the mirror. She looked completely different. It was perfect. Now, she just needed the last touch. She headed out of the dressing room, through the department store, and out into the mall. Bria had removed all the security tags for her, so she made it safely through the store's theft detectors.

Inside the mall, Gena headed to her second stop, a large wig and beauty supply store. She knew exactly which wig she was looking for. It was the one with long braids. She was going for the *How Stella Got Her Groove Back* look.

Gena paid for the wig, walked to the mirror, placed it on her head, and adjusted it until it was just right. Once she was satisfied, she placed her large straw hat on her head and adjusted that too. Next came the sunglasses. Her entire getup was perfect. No one could possibly recognize her. *Shit, I can't even recognize myself.*

Gena headed for a mall exit opposite to the entrance that she had come in. She strolled through the parking lot to a designated parking spot. The car was there, just like they planned; Brianna was on her job. A beige Ford Taurus that Brianna had rented just the day before was sitting in the parking space, with the doors unlocked. Gena climbed inside, lifted the floor mat, and found the key. She stuck the key in the ignition and started the car.

"You muthafuckas ain't the only ones who can pull some 007 shit!" Gena said with a smile. "Shit, fuckin' dead-ass Quadir following me around, like he's fucking crazy. We'll see who's crazy, though. We'll see." She backed the car out of the parking space and headed for her first destination, checking her rearview mirror the entire way. Her plan had worked perfectly; no one had followed her.

Gena's first stop was the Sovereign Bank on Twentieth and Market streets in downtown Center City. This was where she had gotten the safety deposit box and stashed half a million in jewelry. She waited patiently for about twenty minutes before a representative was able to help her. Finally, she was led in through a doorway to the back of the bank. She was seated in a tiny room where her safety deposit box was waiting for her.

"You do have your key?" asked the woman who had assisted her.

"Oh, yeah, it's right here."

Gena waited for the lady to close the door and she slowly unlocked and opened the safety deposit box. It was all there: the ten-karat diamond engagement ring Quadir had proposed to her with; the cluster diamond ring; the birthday charm bracelet that Quadir had given her on the night he threw her party; her diamond initial G pin that Rik and Lita had given her; two Rolexes; one Ebel; one Omega; one Cartier; two gold Gucci watches; one stainless steel and eighteen-karat gold Movado; four tennis bracelets; two-carat diamond earrings; fifteen pairs of gold earrings; and a slew of gold necklaces and bracelets. She removed all of her jewelry and carefully placed each piece side by side as she examined it all carefully. Out of everything in the safety deposit box, there was only one thing she wanted: her ten-karat diamond engagement ring. She slipped the ring on her finger and placed everything else back in the safety deposit box. She closed the lid and locked it.

Her next stop was the Thirtieth Street Station. She pulled up in front of the train station, parking her car at the Market Street side entrance. She took out two suitcases from her trunk and walked through the doors of the train station. She took the escalator down to a lower level where the lockers were located. She looked around and peered back up the escalator just to be sure no one was following her. The coast was clear.

Gena strolled down the row of lockers until she came to hers—405. She inserted the key, opened the door, and looked inside. Her small bundle was sitting just as she had left it. She opened the suitcase, pulled the bag from the locker, and neatly placed it in the suitcase. Lockers 405, 406, 407, 408 all held her secret stash, which totaled a little under $17 million. Once she was done removing the money from each of the lockers and placing it in the suitcases, she walked back down the hall, back up the escalator, and out the side door, carrying with her some $17 million in cold hard cash.

"Whew, that was crazy," she said, once she was in the safety of her car. She looked around as she pulled out of her parking space, careful that she wasn't being followed. This was the most dangerous part of all. For the first time since she had found it, the money was all going to be in one place again.

Her final destination was 4-U-Self Storage, where she could safely count the money she needed for Rik and the money she needed for her great escape, then tuck the rest away in a secure hiding place. She pulled up in front of the storage unit and used her key to open the lock on the unit. Inside were the contents of her house, which she had placed in storage once Viola threw her out into the street. She looked around at all her old furnishings and thought of the life she had once shared with Quadir. She went outside to the car and got the suitcases out of the trunk. She brought them inside the storage unit and closed the door behind her. She looked at the bags of money staring at her and thought of all the trouble the money had caused. *It's not worth it; you're not worth it.* She quickly counted out the money that she needed, the five hundred thousand she planned on giving to Rik. Then she counted out the money that she would take with her. *This is my new-start-at-life money.* Her plan was simple: She would take only what she would need to relocate herself. She had decided that the rest of the money would be safer here, tucked away in the storage unit, than with her.

C.R.E.A.M.

Detective Cleaver stormed up to the table. "How the fuck could you lose her?"

Dick Davis peered up at him. "What?"

"Roscoe P. Coltrane couldn't have fucked this one up! My one-eyed, one-legged grandmother could have kept up with her! She was at a fucking shopping mall!"

Davis rose from the table. Ellington grabbed him.

"You don't know what the fuck you're talking about, asshole!" Davis told Cleaver. "You don't fucking know me! You don't know shit about me!"

"I know that Inspector Clouseau could have done a better job of keeping up with that bimbo!" Cleaver shot back.

"He wasn't on her," Ratzinger told him.

"What?"

"None of my people were on her." Ratzinger repeated. "I had narcotics trailing her."

"What?" Cleaver shouted. "You had those bumbling idiots

shadowing her? They couldn't kept up with their dicks if they weren't attached to their fucking bodies!"

"We needed their manpower and resources," Ratzinger told him.

"Dammit, Ratzinger! I thought we were all in agreement on this. No mistakes, and we keep this as tight as possible!"

"Narcs don't know shit. All they were told was to trail her, and to call me at each stop."

"And she just happened to lose you at her first stop." Cleaver shook his head. "Brilliant, just fucking brilliant. She turned into James fucking Bond and made you look like Gomer fucking Pyle."

"Watch yourself, Sergeant," Ratzinger said sternly.

"Our money just disappeared, Lieutenant."

"Guys, can we put away some of the testosterone here?" Ellington remarked. "This bickering is getting us nowhere. The broad pulled a fast one on us. She thinks she's fucking Harry Houdini, so now we gotta be who we are. We're detectives, so now it's time to hit the street and act like detectives. We find this bitch, and this time we make sure that she doesn't get away from us, that's all."

"We watch her twenty-four-seven," Davis added.

Ellington shook her head. "Naw, we're putting cuffs on this bitch when we find her this time."

"What are we going to charge her with?" Davis asked.

"How about naming her as a suspect in the shooting of her little boyfriend?" Ellington smiled.

"What?" Cleaver was shocked. "What the hell are you talking about, Toya?"

"Her little boyfriend, Jerrell Jackson, was blasted in a motel about a month ago," Ellington explained. "The room was trashed like there had been a struggle and Ms. Scott's prints were all over the place."

"How come nobody said anything about this before?" Cleaver asked.

"Why hasn't Homicide swooped on her?" Ratzinger asked.

"I dug this up only recently. A friend of mine over in Homicide just confirmed everything for me this morning," Ellington told them. "They haven't swooped on her yet because they can't find her. Oh, by the way, she's not a suspect. She's a person of high interest."

"She's not a suspect?" Davis asked incredulously.

Ellington shook her head. "Apparently Homicide is of the opinion that if by some miracle she did do him, it was definitely self-defense. Her blood was all over the room. Her skin was beneath his fingernails, and the victim had bite marks and scratch marks everywhere. And the kicker is, he or she—and they are guessing he—had rope, cement, acid, a saw, and all kinds of macabre shit tucked away in the bathroom."

"Jesus!" Cleaver leaned back and tossed down a drink.

"Evidence suggests that he was going torture her, kill her, and dispose of her body," Ellington told them.

"Torture her? Why torture her?" Davis asked.

"Information," Ratzinger said.

"Information?" Davis lifted an eyebrow.

"He was going to torture her and get her to give up the location of the money," Cleaver said. "Jesus. How many others are after this damn money? This thing's becoming a fucking race to the finish. Like a damn hunt for buried treasure or something."

"We can't put out an all-points bulletin on her, because that's Homicide's job," Ratzinger explained. "People will wonder why vice is putting out an APB for a homicide. It'll raise too many eyebrows. I'll be getting all kinds of calls from vice, from the captain, from everywhere."

Cleaver nodded. "I agree. And we can't alert patrol, because they'll want to know why she's wanted. We have to get out in the streets ourselves."

"We could try to smoke her out," Ratzinger suggested.

"How?" Davis asked.

"Press her grandmother."

"She's in the hospital," Ellington said.

"What for?" Ratzinger asked.

Ellington shook her head. "Another surprise. A gentleman showed up at her door, looking for Gena. When they wouldn't, or couldn't, tell him where she was, he shot the cousin, beat the grandmother, and then raped her."

Cleaver leaned forward. "Raped her?"

Ellington nodded.

Cleaver threw down another drink. "Jesus!"

"Someone else looking for the money?" Ratzinger questioned.

"You think?"

"You don't rape an old woman for kicks," Ratzinger said. "He did it to send a message. He did it to smoke her out."

"How many other people are searching for this girl and this goddamn money?" Cleaver asked. "It'll be like a damn madhouse when someone does find her. Hell, it'll probably be the biggest shootout since D-Day!"

"Sounds like Ms. Gena's days are numbered," Ellington observed.

*　　*　　*

At the Philadelphia Federal Building on Sixth and Market streets in Center City, Agents Phil Covington and Josh Harbinger stood at attention in front of the desk of Special Agent in Charge Rudy Galvani. The SAIC leafed through a small stack of papers with a deep scowl embedded in his face. Finally, he peered up at his agents.

"You bugged the office of a vice lieutenant, two detectives, and an Internal Affairs detective, and you did it without my authorization?" Galvani asked.

"Sir, I thought that I had your consent."

"And what exactly made you think that you had my consent, Agent Harbinger?"

"You gave me permission to see what I could dig up, sir."

"Do you know what professional courtesy is, Agent Harbinger? When we conduct an operation of this nature, it is only professional courtesy to notify the chief of police, and perhaps the local district attorney."

"Sir, the primary target of the operation is a sergeant in the Philadelphia Police Department's Office of Internal Affairs. I didn't know how many others were involved; in fact, I still don't. Sir, what we've uncovered so far involves murder . . ."

Galvani held up his hand, silencing his agent. "I can read. The problem that I have with this operation, Josh, is that I signed off on none of it. You pulled in other field agents, redirected Bureau resources, retasked Bureau assets, and ran roughshod over standard operational procedures. Those procedures are in place for a reason, Agent Harbinger."

"I know, sir. Please, just consider all of the evidence. They're dirty, sir, and they're planning on killing an innocent girl for money."

SAIC Galvani sat and stared at his young agent for several

moments before leaning back in his seat and waving his hand toward the chairs in front of him. "Okay, numb nuts, let's hear it."

A smile spread across Josh's face as he seated himself. Phil wiped away the beads of sweat that were running down his forehead and quickly plopped down into his seat.

"We've got them, sir," Josh said excitedly. "We have recordings of a couple of different conversations. And we've narrowed it down to this small cabal: the vice lieutenant, Cleaver, and the two vice detectives."

"And you knew Cleaver was dirty?"

"Yes, sir."

"All of this time, you've had an itch in your pants for this guy. Why?"

"Sir, when I went undercover as a police detective, he approached me several times to join him in some very questionable activities."

Galvani lifted an eyebrow. "Questionable?"

"Illegal."

Galvani lifted the file and flipped through it again. "Well, it appears you were right about him."

Josh swallowed hard and nodded.

Galvani handed the file back to Harbinger. "If you fart without permission, I'll have you reassigned to the U.S. embassy in Sri Lanka. Do you understand me?"

Josh smiled and nodded.

"Good work, Agent Harbinger. Next time, remember who's the SAIC of this field office."

Josh rose and nodded. "Yes, sir."

Phil also rose.

Galvani lifted his phone and pressed a button. "Sylvia, get

me the district attorney on the telephone, please." He turned to his agents. "You get out, and you make sure you get these crooked sons-a-bitches off the street. You need anything, you call me. You got that?"

Josh nodded. "Yes, sir."

The speakerphone came alive. "Sir, I have United States District Attorney Paul Perachetti on the line."

Galvani lifted the receiver. "Paul, how's it going? You're not going to believe what I have for you today." Galvani covered the receiver. "You two misfits, get the hell outta my office."

Josh and Phil turned and headed for the office door.

"Gentlemen, one last thing," Galvani said.

They stopped and turned back to their boss.

"Don't let them kill her."

Josh nodded and headed out of the office with Phil following close behind.

"I told you he wasn't going to kill us." Josh smiled.

"So, what's next?" Phil asked.

"We make those assholes our new best friends."

"What?"

Josh stopped and turned to his partner. "They are after this money. With a couple of FBI agents hanging around, they're going to get really anxious about trying to get it. They're going to be desperate to make their move, and they're going to do something careless. And when they screw up, we're going to nail their asses to the wall."

"And the girl?"

"They can't touch her with us around."

"How are we going to pull this one off?" Phil asked. "They aren't just going to open their arms and allow us to just hang out with them."

"We become part of the new Federal Vice Task Force."

Phil laughed. "There's no such task force."

"That's never stopped us before. Besides, we know that, but they don't know that. Wherever they are, we will be. I want that bastard Cleaver to make his move."

G

Quadir strolled into the living room and plopped down on the couch. He had just completed an intense workout session in the gym, and yet he still found himself stressed out. Usually working out relaxed him, but today, no matter what he tried, Gena was on his mind.

He had always been there for her when they were together. And he always did whatever was within his power, not just for her, but also for everybody around him. Back then, he could throw money at the problem, he could send some of his boys to fix it, or he could take a quick trip out of town to unwind and relax. None of those things was within his power to do now.

He knew that Gah Git was on Gena's mind. She had always occupied a special place in Gena's heart. Whatever was happening there would be key to making Gena's troubles go away, or at least easing them. And Bria—whatever was going on there would probably work itself out. Teenage drama usually fades with age. And last but not least, the money. Gena had the money, and he knew that she was using it. Whatever problems she had involving money, she was certain to have fixed those by now. The only issue she could be stressing over with the money was whether to give it back. She was probably wondering what she would do if she gave it back.

Quadir leaned back on the couch and began to massage his temples. *I wonder how Cherelle and Quanda are doing.* He had sent his mother to Cherelle to make sure they were okay. Believe it or not, Viola was without a doubt absolutely one hundred percent convinced that Quanda was her granddaughter. And she was nothing but a skeptic, especially when it came to her son.

"Quadir, you can't really believe that this baby of this girl's is yours. She's just looking for a handout. Forget about these chickenheads out there and stay focused, son."

For months and months, Viola had preached the same old sermon, until one day she decided to go off on her own and pay Cherelle a visit.

"Can I help you?" Cherelle asked, standing at the door with Quanda at her side.

"Are you Cherelle Byrd?"

"Who wants to know?" asked Cherelle, not volunteering any information.

"I'm Viola Richards, Quadir's mother. I'm looking for Cherelle Byrd."

"Oh, my God, come in, please. I'm so sorry, I didn't know who you were."

Cherelle opened the screen door for Viola and welcomed her into her first-floor row home apartment. She only had one bedroom for her and Quanda to share, but her apartment was clean, Quanda was clean, and it was clear that Cherelle did the best that she could do for herself and her daughter. She had a sofa and a chair and one floor lamp facing a twenty-eight-inch television sitting on a stand, a small kitchen, an even smaller dinette set, a bathroom, and a bedroom.

"I found your name and address among Quadir's personal things. I tried calling but the number was disconnected."

"I'm glad; I'm glad you came by here," said Cherelle, all smiles, feeling a sense of acceptance for herself and her daughter from Viola. She had yearned to be accepted ever since the birth of her daughter, not only by Quadir, but by his family as well.

"Look, Quanda; look who's here to see you," said Cherelle, introducing Quanda to her grandmother.

"Hi, baby, let me take a good look at you," and Viola meant that shit in every sense of the word.

"This is your grandmom," said Cherelle.

Viola looked piercingly at Cherelle, not appreciating one bit being introduced as the child's grandmother. *That fact remains to be proven.* But the more she looked at the child, the more she saw her own son when he was just a toddler.

"I'm not Grandmom; I'm Granny. You call me Granny, okay?" she said, embracing the little girl as she picked her up and placed her on her lap. "Granny is going to take you shopping and buy you all kinds of toys and clothes, and you and I are going to go to church, how's that?"

Viola looked up and saw a big smile on Cherelle's face. From that point on, there was a bond and a relationship between the two women. Cherelle got exactly what she had always hoped for—Quadir's family's acceptance for her daughter—and Viola got what she wasn't expecting, a granddaughter. By the time Viola was done, she had made up her mind that her grandbaby would never want for anything. From that day forth, if Cherelle needed something, the Richards family had her back.

Quadir smiled as he thought of his mother, Cherelle, and his daughter spending Sunday mornings at church together. He thought of Gena, and the happy smile on his face slowly faded. He could see her now, absolutely disgusted. He could hear her, too.

"Are you crazy? You let your mother throw me to the fucking wolves, while she does everything in her power to make sure Cherelle and your baby are hunky fucking dory?"

Yup, that's about how it would sound. He had decided that just as with Gena, he would have to take care of Cherelle also, once he got his money back. And, of course, Amelia. Gena and Cherelle would both be fine as long as they didn't try to live like rap stars. A million dollars was enough to buy a decent house and car. They would have enough to pay their bills, and Gena could even finish school. She could make a nice life for herself. With a million dollars, Gena could even look out for her grandmother and the rest of her family. God knows, she wouldn't have to work. And just to show how decent he was, he'd put up a million, just in case she needed more at a later date. Maybe ten or twenty years from now, he would shoot her a second mil ticket. That should definitely hold her.

Amelia breezed through the front door.

"Hey."

"Hey yourself!" she said, tossing her keys onto a Bombay chest in the foyer. She sat her briefcase down next to it, strolled into the living room, and kissed Quadir on his cheek. "Whatcha doing?"

Quadir shook his head.

"Why so glum?" she asked.

"Just doing some thinking."

"About?"

"Money, Gena, all of that stuff."

"You seem to never stop thinking about her. Actually, it seems as though she's the only thing you ever do think of."

Quadir peered up. "How do you figure?"

"Oh, Quadir, please. It's true."

Quadir looked away. He wasn't quite sure what he was supposed to say. In a way, Amelia was right. She was all he thought of, her and his money. He often wondered whether, if she didn't have his money, he would ever have thoughts of her.

"You know I didn't tell you this, but remember the night you brought Gena here? Well, when I examined her, I realized that she had suffered a miscarriage."

"She was . . . pregnant."

"Yeah, she lost the baby, though. I guess Jerrell beat her so bad, she lost it."

Silence fell and a look of despair fell upon Quadir's face.

"Are you okay?" Amelia asked.

The last thing he wanted to hear was that Gena had been pregnant by Jerrell.

"I said are you okay?" Amelia asked again, realizing for the first time just how deep his concentration was set in Gena mode.

He still loves her. Amelia realized the truth of the matter. She had never thought in a million years that hearing Gena had a miscarriage would even remotely affect him. She honestly thought that his hearing that piece of information would drive him further away from her, and he'd let it go, let her go,

even let the money go. However, his reaction indicated that he
wasn't about to let anything go.

"Quadir, I can't do this anymore," said Amelia in almost a
hushed tone.

"Can't do what?"

"I can't pretend. Maybe you can, but I can't."

"Amelia, what are you talking about?"

"I'm talking about you, me, you and me. It's nothing, it's
just make pretend. You pretend to have feelings for me that
you just don't have, and I sit here and pretend that maybe, just
maybe you'll forget about her, and love me. But the truth is
you won't, and I'm tired of pretending that maybe you will."

"Are you saying that I'm in love with Gena?"

"I don't have to say it. Why does anyone have to say it? I
mean, my God, it's written all over your face," said Amelia.
"She needs you, Quadir."

"Doc, I don't understand."

"That's your problem, Quadir. You always want to try to
figure things out, you always want to try to dissect, to label, to
understand and rationalize. Some things are not meant to be
understood. Some things are, because they just are. You love
her, she loves you, and right now, she needs you more than
ever."

"And what about us?"

"What about us?" Amelia asked with a smile on her face.
"Maybe we are meant to be together, maybe we aren't, maybe
it's just . . . bad timing, maybe in another life. I don't know.
But, I know this; you need to help her. You are the only one
who can."

"Yeah, but . . ."

"But nothing, Quadir. I'm here, you know, and besides, you

don't stop loving someone, Quadir. In fact, if it's true love, it never really ends. It changes, it grows deeper, more profound, it morphs into different manifestations, but it's always there. True love lasts through time and space and distance." Amelia paused for a moment, hearing her own words as a tear whelped in her eye. "She loved you, even when you were on the other side. You think that I'll stop loving you, just because you are across the country?"

"I thought that we were going to go across the country together."

"Sometimes, people are meant to travel this life together for great distances, sometimes short ones."

"And you and me?"

"Who said that our journey together is over? Who knows what the future holds for us, Quadir? But right now, what we do know is that Gena needs you."

"And you don't need me?" Quadir looked down.

"No, I don't need you," Amelia said, knowing that deep, deep, down inside she wished, dreamed, and even prayed for Quadir to be for her. However, no matter how much she prayed and wished on one hundred four-leaf clovers, he wasn't. And she knew in her heart that she deserved better. She deserved someone for her, someone who would be just for her.

Of course I need you, and of course I want you. And I have been blessed to have you in my life. But I need one hundred per-cent of you, you know, not half of you, because the other half is still somewhere in the past. Amelia caressed the side of his face. Maybe she should have spoken those words, but she didn't, and she wasn't going to. She'd rather he thought the opposite than know that she was truly and deeply brokenhearted.

"I really think that you need to go to her. You need to work everything out with her, and then if you're sure, sure that your heart is free and you're sure you want to be with me, then I'll be here. But not like this. Not like this. Not with all this hanging over your head."

"I love you," he said as he leaned forward and kissed her on her cheek. "I owe you my life. I owe you more than words can express."

"You owe me nothing, Quadir. The only person you owe is yourself. We get one shot at this game called life. One shot. And we have to take that one chance and live it to the fullest. Enjoy every fucking waking moment of it. Never let a sunrise go by without appreciating it and being thankful for a new day. Never walk by a pot of food without tasting it, and never walk by a flower without stopping to smell it."

Quadir smiled and rose.

"You go and save Gena, you hear me? It's the right thing to do."

Quadir nodded.

"Wait a minute, before you go." Amelia rose and rushed down the hall to her bedroom. She was gone for several moments before she returned. She handed Quadir a black .40-caliber Glock pistol and several loaded clips. "I know, I know. I'm a doctor, what the hell am I doing with that? Well, I'm also a single black woman living alone."

Quadir shook his head and smiled. "Doc, I have never in life met anyone like you."

Amelia nodded and smiled. "I know. My daddy says that I'm crazy, but I get it from his side of the family. Hey, you go and find that girl. You find her, and you two get the hell outta this place. I don't want to hear from you again until you're safe. You understand?"

Quadir nodded.

"Unless of course you need me, and if you ever need me, you know where to find me. That Glock has a twin right in my closet, and I'll bust a muthafucka's ass if I have to. I'll have to try to save the son of a bitch after I shoot him, but that won't stop me from pulling the trigger!"

Quadir laughed, leaned forward, and kissed her on her cheek again, before turning and heading for the front door.

"One game," Amelia shouted. "The only game that matters; the game of life. Be true to that game, Qua. Be true to the game!"

GOOSE CHASE

Who is it?" Markita shouted.

"It's me!"

"Me who?"

"Me!"

Markita opened her front door to find a stranger standing before her. "May I help you?"

Terrell smiled. "Hey, baby, why you look so disappointed?"

Markita smiled, but wasn't for the bullshit. If it wasn't for the fact that the nigga was tall, dark, and handsome, she would have slammed the door in his face. *I ain't hardly disappointed,* Markita thought, wondering who he was and what he wanted.

"Were you expecting someone else?" Terrell asked.

"No." Markita smiled. "I'm not expecting anybody, but you gonna have to come on, 'cause *The Young and the Restless* is on."

"Damn, it's like that?"

"Like what? What do you want?"

"Well, I'm a friend of Gena's, and she told me she was staying here. I just wanted to drop by and see how she was doing and check on her, you know, see if she needed anything."

Immediately, Markita let her guard down, not realizing that the handsome stranger standing in front of her was the enemy who had been hunting Gena, not the friend he was pretending to be.

"Oh, Gena, she's not here right now. You want me to tell her you stopped by?"

"Yeah, that would be great. Do you think you can take my number down and have her call me?" asked Terrell.

"Yeah, sure, let me get a pen."

And that was it right there. Markita turned from the doorway, took two steps, grabbed a pen off the coffee table, and turned around to find Terrell standing right behind her, her front door closed.

"What are you doing? I didn't invite you in."

"I invited myself," said Terrell, as he began to unzip his pants and fondle himself in front of Markita.

"Oh, my God! Help!" screamed Markita as she tried to run. She made a dash for her bedroom and slammed the door shut, locking it simultaneously. She picked up the telephone receiver and dialed 911. But as the phone rang, Terrell busted through her bedroom door, saw her with the phone in her hand, and snatched it away, disconnecting the call as he slapped Markita so hard she fell back on the bed and then onto the floor. Desperately, she began to crawl across her bedroom floor, but Terrell was on top of her just as she reached her bedroom doorway.

"Where you going? The party's just about to begin."

"*Heeellpppp!*" Markita screamed.

"Shut the fuck up," said Terrell as he punched her head, grabbed her by her throat, and yanked her off the floor. "If you fucking scream I'll kill you, do you understand me? Do you understand me?" he hollered like a maniac in her ear.

"Yes, yes, I understand; please don't hurt me."

"You do what I say, everything I say, and I might let you live."

"Okay, okay," said Markita as she felt him letting go of her neck.

"Take your clothes off."

Markita didn't know what to do. She was standing there desperately trying to think of something, something to do or something to say, that would get her out of the situation she was in.

"What the fuck is you standing there for?" said Terrell as he savagely attacked her, pushing her onto the bed and ripping at her clothes.

Markita tried to fight him, she tried to use her strength, but Terrell was physically stronger, and he hit Markita again, this time on her face, immediately swelling her eye, and it was then that Markita stopped fighting. She let him have his way. As he pulled at her clothes and ripped off her pants, she simply lay there imagining it all as a bad dream.

Terrell raped Markita repeatedly, pinning her down, holding the back of her neck as she lay on her stomach. Then he pulled out of Markita and quickly reinserted himself into her other hole. Markita almost leaped from the bed, but Terrell grabbed her arms and held her tightly. She screamed at the top of her lungs.

"Oh, God, please, no, stop, please no!" she screamed as Terrell ripped into her. She could feel the wetness and suspected that she was bleeding. The only sound besides her cries, was Terrell's grunting. He sounded like a wild animal.

"Stop it!" Markita screamed. "Please, help, please, stop!"

Terrell held her arms in place and continued to brutalize her anus.

"Stop it, please!"

More grunting.

"Help me, please!" she screamed louder.

Grunting.

"Help me!"

Grunting.

"Somebody help me, please!"

More grunting, followed by a wild cry of carnal pleasure as Terrell exploded inside her asshole. His thrusting and throbbing caused her to let out a blood-curdling cry.

"Shut up! Shut up! You fucking whore, you know you like it."

Terrell continued to breathe heavily, trying to regain his expended energy. "Markita."

It was then that she realized he knew her name, and she had never told it to him.

"I have a question for you. And I need for you to be really honest with me."

"What?"

"I need you to call Gena for me and I need you to tell her to come over here."

"What?" Markita again tried to force her way out from under Terrell. He gripped her arms tightly.

"You heard me; I need you to call Gena and tell her to come over here. You probably will have to make it sound like an emergency or something."

"How the fuck am I supposed to do that? I don't even know where she is. I don't even know how to reach her."

"Tell me where I can find her."

"I don't know!"

"Where can I find her?"

"I don't know!"

"Don't lie to me, Markita," Terrell said. "I know that she lives here."

"Gena don't live here!" Markita struggled to break free. "I don't know where you got your information from, but they telling you wrong! Gena used to live in the apartment next door, but that was long ago!"

"Her cousin said that you two live together."

"Her cousin lied!"

"Why would she lie to me?"

"Who the fuck knows! Get off of me!"

"Tell me where I can find Gena."

"I don't know. I swear I don't know, and if I did, I wouldn't fucking tell you anyway," Markita screamed at the top of her lungs.

Terrell scooped her up and wrapped his massive arms around Markita's neck. He kissed the back of her neck and licked her around to the right side of her ear, and then twisted in one quick, forceful motion. Her neck sounded like a dry twig when it snapped.

Terrell remained on top of her as her body spasmed and convulsed. Once he was finished, he climbed off her and began to search her apartment for evidence of Gena's whereabouts. Gena had lots of clothing in Markita's apartment, some of which she had worn recently. It was in an older pair of pants that Terrell found what he was looking for, however. It was a business card for 4-U-Self Storage.

FINDERS KEEPERS

Gena knocked on the door more forcefully the second time; still no answer. Markita was known for hopping into the shower or getting lost in a damn soap opera and simply tuning out the rest of world. *Oh, come on, Kita, I got to use the bathroom, girl.*

Gena knocked once again and then twisted the doorknob to see if the door was unlocked. The knob turned. *The door was open all along.* She pushed open the front door and crept into the apartment.

"Markita."

No answer.

The television was on, as were most of the lights. The apartment looked to be even messier than usual, which wasn't saying a lot, because Markita's house was always junky. Gena made her way into the bedroom. It was dark, as the bedroom shades and curtains were drawn, and sure enough, Markita was lying in bed.

"Girl, get your ass up. What are you still doing in bed? We

got things to do; come on, I need your help," said Gena as she tapped on her girlfriend's shoulder. Markita felt cold.

"Markita?"

No answer.

Gena pushed her friend more forcefully, causing the blankets to move. The dried bloodstain over Markita's butt became visible. Gena covered her mouth.

"Markita!" Gena shook her friend. "Markita. Oh, my God!" Gena pushed Markita over, to find herself looking into her friend's open but lifeless eyes.

"Markita!" Gena grabbed her friend's wrist and felt for a pulse. There was none. "Oh, my God! Oh, my God!" Gena backed against a wall, where she slid down to the floor and burst into tears. She knew what had happened. Whoever had hurt Gah Git had now killed her closest friend. *He must have been looking for me.* Yes, the crazy man had gone there looking for her, and Markita had paid the price. He had done to her what he had done to Gah Git, but even worse. Gah Git still had some life left in her after he had gone, whereas Markita had none.

Gena wiped away the tears that were pouring down her face. She had lost another best friend, another friend to bullshit. It was the city. The city was taking life away from her, slowly but steadily. It was closing in on her. It was out to get her. She had to get away, she had to run for her life. If not, she too would be dead soon. She could feel it coming. Death was around the corner, and it was creeping toward her. Slowly but surely death was tracking her down.

Gena willed herself to rise. She kissed Markita's dead, cold, lifeless cheek. She was out of there. *Fuck Philly, fuck Richard Allen, fuck Quadir, fuck my entire life.* Gena was done; she was ready to go and never, ever look back. Philly had taken her parents, it had taken Sahirah, it had taken Quadir away from her, it had taken Markita, it almost took Gah Git and Gary, and it was about to take Bria and herself, if she didn't do something about it.

Gena moved away from Markita's corpse and made her way out to the living room. *Should I call the police? Just to get someone here? God, she'll be lying here all alone for days if I don't call. I have to do something. But what, what should I do?* Before leaving, Gena called 911 and reported the finding of a dead body. She remained anonymous, and immediately hung up the phone after giving the operator Markita's address. Gena headed down the steps to the front porch of Markita's house and climbed into her rental. She had to get out of town, and she had to go tonight. She would meet with Rik, square him away, stash her cash, and then leave this place for good. She was heading south, maybe Norfolk, maybe Charleston, maybe Charlotte, maybe even Atlanta. She would know once she got there. The only thing she knew for certain was that she was going tonight. Her life depended on it.

Cornell Cleaver stepped under the yellow police lines and made his way into the apartment. He flashed his badge at the uniformed police officer guarding the door and was allowed to pass.

"What the fuck is IAD doing here?" Detective Smith shouted from across the room. "Nobody's fucked shit up yet."

"Curtis Miles!" Cleaver smiled. He walked to where the homicide detectives were standing and shook his friend's hand. "It's been a long time."

"What's your ugly face doing here?" Miles asked.

"Just passing through," Cleaver told him.

"Passing through, huh?" Miles asked suspiciously. "Bullshit. Whose balls are you trying to break? IAD doesn't crawl out of its little cubicle unless it's trying to bust balls."

Cleaver lifted his hands and shrugged. "I'm just passing through, Curtis. Honest to goodness."

Miles waved to the gentleman standing next to him. "This is Detective Harmon Brittingham. He's one of my best detectives, and he's going to be the lead detective on this case. Harm, this here is Cleaver; he's IAD. Used to work for me in Homicide, used to work for me in Vice before that, used to work Narcotics before that. He used to be a real cop once, and now he's a ball buster."

"You flatter me with your kind words, Lieutenant," Cleaver told him.

"You come here to fuck with my guys, you let me know," Miles told him with a "don't fuck with me either" look on his face. "Those are the rules of the game. You don't fuck with my guys without me knowing about it, you got that?"

Cleaver nodded. "Where's the victim?"

"She's in the bedroom." Miles peered up at the door. "Holy fuck, what the fuck we got going on here, a convention? This is a homicide investigation, not a goddamn policemens' ball! What do you two numb nuts want here?"

Cleaver turned and spied Ellington and Davis making their way toward them.

"What the fuck is vice doing here?" Miles asked.

"We heard that she was connected," Ellington told him.

"I haven't heard that," Miles shot back.

"You're Homicide, not Vice, so you wouldn't have heard that, now would you?" Ellington asked in an aloof tone of voice.

"Letoya, you're looking mighty tasty as usual."

"And you're still looking desperate, Lieutenant."

"How's your mother?"

"Good, since she's never met you."

Lieutenant Miles threw back his head in laughter. "I see your tongue is still sharp."

"And I see that your belly's getting rounder. Picking up some weight, are we?" Ellington placed her hand over Miles's stomach and giggled at his belly.

"Watch it. Moves like that make it turn hard."

"How would you know?" Ellington smiled. "You haven't seen that shriveled little piece of meat since Nixon was in the White House."

The detectives and officers around the room laughed heartily.

"What we got here?" Davis asked, peeking through the bed-room door.

"Female, black, early twenties, death by strangulation, looks like. Coroner's on his way; we'll know more then," Harmon Brittingham explained. "You wanna see some weird shit?"

The detectives followed Brittingham into the bedroom. He pulled back the covers, displaying Markita's naked body. "She got fucked in the ass, probably right before her death."

"Or perhaps even during," Ellington suggested.

"Sick bastard," Cleaver chimed in.

"Judging from the amount of blood, it wasn't something that she did on a regular basis," Brittingham advised.

"Raped?" Davis asked.

Harmon Brittingham shook his head. "Doesn't look like a forced entry. No pun intended. No forced entry into the apartment either."

"She knew the perp," Cleaver added.

Brittingham shrugged. "Apparently. It looks like the sex was consensual. I mean from what I can tell, she let the guy in, she's not bruised or beaten, so it looks as if she voluntarily had sex. But something went wrong. No telling what made it turn bad."

"The apartment looks like it's been ransacked," Ellington observed.

"Talked to the neighbors, and apparently the victim kept a pretty messy apartment," Brittingham explained.

"Any leads?" Cleaver asked.

"Forensics are on their way. We got semen, tissue maybe, definitely skin cells, sweat, perhaps some hair. All the usual trace elements from sexual intercourse," Brittingham advised.

"Whoever did this doesn't give a fuck if he's caught," Davis observed.

"He's probably not planning on being in town long enough to give a shit about any evidence," Ellington said.

"All right, spill it!" Miles ordered, watching Ellington and Davis summarize a case, although he had no clue what they were summarizing.

"What?" Ellington asked.

"What the fuck are you working on that made you show up here today? And how did you come to the conclusion that this son of a bitch is planning to skip town? I want to know what you know, Detective, and I want to know now!" Miles said forcefully.

"Remember the assault on the old lady that happened last month sometime?" Ellington asked. "The really brutal one?"

Miles scratched his head as he tried to remember. "I think I do. The old woman from the projects. She was raped. Fucked in the . . ."

"Jesus!" Brittingham whistled. "Same fucking MO. You think they're related?"

Ellington nodded. "I know they are. The girl that he was looking for when he attacked the old lady was her best friend," said Ellington, pointing to Markita's dead, naked body.

"Why in the fuck didn't you say so when you first walked in?" Miles shouted. "What, is this a fucking poker game or something? We holding our cards close, Detective?"

"What the fuck does Vice have to do with any of this?" Brittingham asked.

"The girl's husband was a major dealer who got popped. He was a Vice target. She was also a Vice target. Her new boyfriend popped her husband; he was a major dealer, and a Vice target, and then he got popped," Ellington explained.

"Who'd he get popped by, her third boyfriend?" Miles proclaimed. "Talk about some bad-luck pussy."

"So who are we after here?" Brittingham asked, just wanting his job to be as simple as possible.

Ellington shrugged. "I wish we knew. The only thing we do know is that this guy is a fucking nut case."

"I want the file on this one," Miles told her. "I want to know everything that you know, and I want to know it yesterday. I'm getting this son of a bitch off the streets."

Two dark-suited men stepped into the bedroom. They were young, clean-shaven, well-dressed. They screamed Feds.

"And you two are?" Miles asked, not playing any more games with his crime scene.

"I am Agent Harbinger, and this is my colleague, Agent Covington. We're from the Federal Bureau of Investigation."

"FBI?" Miles huffed. "What's your jurisdiction here?"

"Excuse me?" Josh asked.

"Well, we got Homicide, Internal Affairs, and now FBI. I guess DEA and Customs will show up next, telling me that she was smuggling for the cartel. This whole thing stinks to high heaven. Why are so many noses interested in a young, dead black woman with no criminal record, no known boyfriends, vices, or any other red flags in her history? Why is the FBI here, at a homicide scene? Don't tell me: She was kidnapped at the age of four? You heard me, why are you here?"

Josh smiled. "Was she a victim of an abduction?"

"Don't get cute with me, son!" Miles bellowed. "What's the FBI's business here? I'm trying to conduct a homicide investigation."

"We're conducting a highly classified federal investigation," Josh told him. "We're going to take a look around, if you don't mind. By the way, why did you say you had vice detectives here?"

"I didn't."

"Why are they here?" Phil asked Josh. He removed a notepad and pen from his pocket.

"And why is Internal Affairs here?" Josh added.

"Just leaving," Cleaver told them. He stormed from the room angrily. *Fucking FBI. I needed a chance to search the damn place and these assholes show up. Fuck! I'll have to come back later when the circus is over.*

Ellington and Davis headed for the exit.

"I'll get those files to you, Lieutenant," Ellington told him as she left the apartment.

Phil and Josh turned to each other and smiled.

"You wanna tell me what's going on here?" Miles asked, looking at Harbinger and Covington as the room cleared out.

"Hey, we just wanted to jump-start the marathon," joked Josh as he patted Covington on the back.

"Yeah, get 'em up and runnin'."

LET'S CALL IT A COMEBACK

Michael pulled up his Lincoln Navigator in front of Gah Git's house. His mother looked somewhat tired.

"You okay?" he asked as he placed his hand on top of hers.

"Yes, son, yes, I'm fine. You gonna have to help me out this big truck you got," Gah Git said.

"I'll help you, Gah Git," said Bria, hopping out and opening the door for her grandmother.

"Here, I got her," said Michael, pushing Bria out of the way to assist his mother.

"Dag, Uncle Michael, just push me down the next time," joked Bria.

"Come on, Mama; don't pay her no mind."

"That crazy child right there, is you kiddin' me?" added Gah Git, agreeing with her son.

"Whatever, say what you want, you know who be in here taking care of you, Gah Git. Uncle Michael's just a visitor, Gah Git. I'm the one who's gonna have to take care of you."

"Lord have mercy, I'll be all tore up in here with you and

your crazy sister," said Gah Git as she looked at her grand-daughter and thought of Irene, the twins' mother, who had died while giving birth to the girls. Gah Git thought of her daughter, Irene, every day. Everybody did, but no one talked of the twins' mother, no one really ever said Irene's name, never. That's how Gah Git had ended up with the twins. Gah Git brought them home from the hospital and went over to the funeral home the next day and buried her daughter. Gwendolyn's crazy ass was too busy doing other things, like getting high, to take care of Khaleer, so Gah Git demanded the youngster stay with her. And when Gwendolyn had Brandi, addicted to crack cocaine at birth, Gah Git stepped in and took her from Social Services. Ms. Bradley, the social worker assigned to Brandi's case, still came by from time to time just to visit with Gah Git. She had been trying to get Gah Git to foster mother some abandoned children in the system, but Gah Git had her hands full. Paula was the only child of hers who seemed to have it together. She worked at the bank as an assistant branch manager, she dated on and off, took her yearly vacations to the Caribbean, and was raising Gary, Zorian, and Avanna on her own.

Michael swung open the door as Bria held the screen door for Gah Git. Out of nowhere, the darkened living room lit up and all the family popped out of nowhere.

"*Surprise!*"

Everyone yelled in unison as Gah Git stepped through the door. Gah Git looked around the room at her family and thought her eyes were playing tricks on her. There were "welcome home" balloons and ribbons, and flowers from neighbors and well-wishers filled the tiny living room. Paula had cooked for two days and two nights, and if you didn't know better, you would have thought it was Thanksgiving.

"Malcolm? Malcolm, is that you?"

"Yeah, Mama, they done let a black man be free."

"Malcolm, oh, son; I can't believe it." Gah Git used every bit of strength she had in her and embraced her son. It had been so long since she had seen him. Tears rolled down her checks.

"I been praying, son, praying that you would come home. I'm just so glad you're here. You just don't know," she said, still cradling her firstborn son in her arms.

"Yes, Malcolm, that's all she's been talking about: you coming home. We're glad to see you," said Paula, giving her older brother a hug as Gah Git finally passed him over.

Gah Git's heart lit up like the Christmas tree in Rockefeller Plaza as all her grandbabies ran over to her.

"You been sleeping in that bathtub, boy," said Gah Git, joking with Khaleer.

"No." He laughed at her, knowing darn well that he had been.

"Yeah, brother; good to see you," said Gwendolyn, looking as if she had partied like a rock star all night long as she gave her brother a long embrace.

"Yeah, man, congratulations on coming home," said Royce, extending his hand. It didn't take a rocket scientist to figure out that his sister and Royce had a habit, a bad habit. Maybe later he would talk to her about it. Let her know that no matter what, he had her back.

"Come on, Mama," he said, helping Michael get Gah Git over to the couch.

"Look who's here, your grandbaby Gary," said Michael as he moved Gary's wheelchair over to his grandmother.

"You can't walk, Gary?" said Gah Git as she noticed the

wheelchair and was about to get upset that no one had told her.

"Of course he can walk, Gah Git. We stole that chair from the hospital and brought it home for you. So, this way, we can roll you around," said Brianna, bending over and kissing Gah Git on the face.

"Mmm-hmm, roll me around all right. I can see you rolling me too, right down a flight of stairs."

"Gah Git, nuh-uh, we love you," said Bria, standing next to her sister.

"Hey, brother, we got to talk. I got some big things planned out for you," said Michael as he patted his older brother on the back.

"Yeah?" Malcolm replied.

"Hell yeah, don't worry, big brother; you gonna be just fine, just fine and dandy."

Malcolm looked around the room at all his family. Their smiling faces and warm embraces and love filled him with joy. He didn't know what to say. Everyone acted as if nothing had happened. Michael had visited him many, many times. He knew his brother had forgiven him a long, long time ago. He thought of all the time he had missed, all the time that had passed him by. He was just glad to be home. At first he was scared, but when he saw his little brother waiting for him outside those prison gates, he knew everything would be okay. He knew he'd be all right. He looked at his family, laughing, joking, eating, and sharing one another's company. Just about everyone was there—everyone except Gena.

Gena pulled up to the motel room and extinguished her head-lights. She saw Rik peeking out through blinds as she parked her car. It made her smile, and she waved back to him. She looked around the parking lot. Rik's car was parked out in front where she could easily see it. Unknown to her, Rik and Quadir used to meet at this same hotel back in the day when they did business. Rik had chosen the motel for sentimental reasons.

Gena turned off the ignition, climbed out, and headed for the motel room with the plastic bag of money in her hand. She imagined what it must have been like to do a dope deal. All of the sneaking around, the intrigue, the secret locations, the peeking out of the windows. They acted like they were James Bond or something.

Rik opened the motel room door and embraced her tightly. "Hey, baby girl!"

"Hey, Rik." Gena hugged him.

"How have you been?"

Gena shook her head and then burst into tears. "It's too much, you know. I'm just going through it. You just don't know what I'm going through."

"What's the matter?" Rik asked.

"Markita, my friend, something bad happened to her."

"What's going on?"

"She's dead. I just found her body," Gena blurted out. Her tears fell more rapidly.

Rik wrapped his arms around her. "I'm so sorry to hear that."

Gena wrapped her arms around Rik and began bawling. "And Gah Git, my grandmom, someone beat her and raped her, Rik. She's still in the hospital. And my cousin Gary tried to save her, and the guy shot Gary, and Bria's boyfriend."

"Who?"

Gena shook her head. "I don't know. He's trying to kill me. They all said the same thing, that this guy is looking for me."

Rik pulled her close and walked her into the motel room. He shut the door and locked it. "Gena, what's going on? Why would someone be trying to kill you?"

Again, she shook her head. "I don't know."

"You have no idea?"

Gena shook her head. "I don't even know what he looks like. He just showed up one day asking where I was and started attacking people."

"But why you? Why now? Why all of a sudden? What do you have that he would want?"

Gena pulled away. "I don't know, Rik! He just showed up. Why are you questioning me like this?"

"Gena, you offered me a lot of money when I was in jail."

"So?"

"Is he after the money?"

Gena shook her head. "I don't know."

"Where did you get that kinda money?" Rik asked. "And be honest with me, Gena."

"What does it matter where the money comes from? What difference does it make?" Gena lifted the plastic bag and tossed it to Rik. "Here's the money you asked me for."

She turned and headed for the door. Rik grabbed her.

"Gena, did you find Qua's money?"

"Rik, let go of me!" Gena yanked her arm away and unlocked the door. Rik pulled her back.

"Gena, do you have Quadir's money?" Rik asked more forcefully.

"Rik, let me go! What the hell is wrong with you?"

Rik slung Gena back onto the bed. Gena fell onto the bed

and rolled off onto the floor. *This shit can't be happening again. Not again; not Rik!* She rose and charged at Rik, digging her nails into his eyes. Rik howled, pulled her hands out of his face, and backhanded her. Gena stumbled back a few steps, then raced for the door. This time, she was able to get it open before he grabbed her.

"Help me!" Gena screamed. "Somebody help me!"

"Shut up and just tell me where the rest of the money is," Rik shouted. He slung Gena onto the bed and tried to kick the motel room's door closed. The door flew back open. Rik turned to see what was blocking the door. Quadir was standing in the doorway.

Rik's eyes bulged from their sockets and he backed up into the room

Gena jumped onto Rik's back. He flipped her off him onto the floor.

"Son of a bitch!" Gena shouted. She spat at Rik, missing him by a couple of feet.

"Now, now, Rik. Is that any way to treat a lady?" Quadir asked. He leaned forward and helped Gena up. "Especially your best friend's girl?"

Rik reached for his weapon, but Quadir already had his drawn.

"Uh-uh, don't even think about it," Quadir told him, pointing his Glock at his friend.

"You sorry muthafucka!" Gena tried to go at Rik again, but Quadir held her back.

"Quadir, what the fuck is going on here?" Rik asked nervously. "What the fuck's going on? This ain't right, man. This shit ain't right."

"What's not right is trying to rob Gena for my dough, nigga. Now, that ain't right," Quadir told him.

"Qua, man, this is some twisted shit. I saw you, Ock. I went to your funeral. I was a pallbearer. This ain't no real shit."

Quadir nodded. "Oh, yeah, I'm real all right, which is a whole lot more than I can say about you, Ock."

Rik shook his head. "Man, you not understanding. I'm doing bad, Qua. Them Santero motherfuckers is going to kill me, man. If I don't give them they bread by yesterday, I'm a dead man."

Gena tried to spit on Rik again. "I was going to give you the money, you son of a bitch!"

"This ain't enough, Gena!"

"I woulda given you anything you asked for!" Gena shouted.

"So, you were going to do Gena in?" Quadir asked. "Instead of being a brother to her, and protecting her, and helping her, you were going to kill her and take the money that I left for her? Damn, nigga, that's some fucked-up shit. I can't believe you."

Tears fell from Rik's eyes. "Quadir, you were dead! And she had already moved on! She moved right on to the next dope boy. She wasn't coming around us no more; she wasn't being part of the family! She started fucking with that same nigga that did you! What the fuck, Qua? She wasn't family no more, and she had betrayed you with them Junior Mafia muthafuckas!"

"Regardless, you ready to kill her, Rik?" Quadir asked.

"She betrayed you, Ock! For all we know, she set you up for them niggas! She could have been setting you up the whole time! Qua, she's brand-new to the game! But me and you, we go back to the sandbox, homie! It was us who used to be break dancing up in my yard on cardboard boxes; it was us who got our first piece together! It's me, black."

The three of them turned toward the window when they saw the flashing red and blue lights outside. Gena raced to the window and peered outside. The patrolman was walking into the motel room office.

"It's just one car," Gena told him. "Somebody probably called about the disturbance."

"I got a plan, Quadir," Rik told him. "I got a connect who's willing to send us so much snow, it'll be like January the whole year around. All I need is the money to square up what I owe. After that, they cut on the faucet, and the dope runs like water. We just set up another crew and rake in the bread."

Quadir clasped Gena's hand and shook his head. "Thanks, but no thanks."

"Quadir, what is you doing? I need that money!" Rik shouted.

Gena lifted the bag of money off the floor.

"Don't tell me you not down, Quadir. I know you, nigga, I know how you get down for that paper, homie. Come on, baby boy, ride with me. I'm your brother, Ock. You gonna let me die, Qua? What part of the game is that?" asked Rik, not realizing that Quadir was going to murder him himself.

"Qua, we gotta go," Gena said softly. She pulled him toward the door.

"Whatever happened to being true to that game?" Rik shouted.

Gena opened the motel room door.

"I need that money, Qua!"

"Rik, don't."

"I need that money!"

"Rik, don't!"

"I need that fucking money!" Rik reached for his weapon.

Quadir squeezed the trigger of his weapon several times, sending Rik flying back onto the bed. Just as the gunshots rang through the silent night air, the officer ran out of the motel office. Gena yanked him out of the motel room, and they raced through the parking lot toward her car. The officer spotted them, Gena with a bag of drug money and Quadir with a loaded weapon in his hand.

"No, we'll never make it past that cop!" Quadir shouted. He yanked her in the opposite direction. "My car is parked around back!"

"Freeze!" yelled the officer, and without hesitation began shooting at his runaway targets. *What the fuck? This guy is trying to kill me, not capture me,* Quadir thought as a bullet skimmed right by him. He could feel the bullets in the air zooming by him as he made his escape. As they made their way through the dark parking lot, they wove and ducked as the officer aimed directly for them.

Quadir and Gena raced around the rear of the motel, disappearing as the police officer ran over to his squad car and yelled through the radio for backup.

The race was now on. They both had to get out of town, and they had to do it tonight—Gena because she had a killer lurking somewhere in the city desperate to find her, and Quadir because he had just murdered his best friend in a motel room.

Gena climbed inside Quadir's black Range Rover, and they raced down the street. She peered out the window, thinking about how many other lives would be lost because of that fucking money. She wished that it would all just burn to ashes.

"I loved him like a brother," Quadir said softly.

"I know," Gena told him. She placed her hand on top of his. "I did too. I never thought he would hurt me though."

For the first time in a long time, she and her man were together once again, helping each other, comforting each other, and being down for each other. For the first time in a long time, the old Quadir and Gena were back.

CRIME SCENE 101

Davis strolled into the motel room, followed by Ellington. Lieutenant Miles rose from his knee and gave them a cynical smile.

"Well, well, well, here we go again. A regular fucking family reunion we're having. You two keep showing up at my crime scenes; I'm going to have you reassigned to homicide. So, what gives this time?"

Ellington and Davis exchanged glances.

"Don't tell me, he was the other victim's long-lost uncle, who also happened to be a coke dealer whom you were investigating."

"He was our CI," Davis told him.

"He was a confidential informant for Vice. Well, isn't that just convenient. Could that be the reason that he's no longer with us? I wonder. I mean, working for a couple of numb nuts like you two could definitely get somebody killed."

"Lieutenant, may we take a look around?" Ellington asked.

"Don't disturb anything; don't touch anything. Forensics has just started their work."

Ellington nodded. "Anybody check his pockets?"

Miles shook his head. "Forensics will handle it. He was DOA when the first officer arrived on the scene. Seems there was a disturbance call about the room. So a patrolman was already at the motel office when the shooting went down."

"Do we have anyone in custody?" Ellington asked excitedly.

Miles shook his head. "The police officer ran out of the front office when he heard gunshots. He exchanged gunfire with the assailant before the assailant fled the scene. The police officer called for backup, then ran in here to the motel room, found the victim, tried CPR, and had someone call the paramedics. The police officer says that he couldn't resuscitate the victim, so he immediately secured the room."

"Which was rented to?" Davis asked.

"The victim."

"What kinda commotion?" Ellington asked.

"A huge brawl. Thumping, crashing, banging, screaming, shouting."

"Screaming? Like a woman screaming?"

Miles nodded. "You got it."

"Any eyewitnesses?" Ellington asked.

"We're running down leads right now, but besides the officer, none," Miles told them. "And since you two are so interested in this case, why don't you make yourselves useful and go and help interview some of the motel guests and see if anyone saw or heard anything?"

Ellington and Davis exchanged glances.

"And I want to know everything you find out," Miles hollered.

Agents Covington, Harbinger, and Stokes strolled into the motel room.

"Well, well, well," Miles shook his head and smiled. "Last time I checked, Philadelphia was not part of the District of Columbia, so murders here are within the jurisdiction of the state."

"Right you are about that, Lieutenant." Harbinger smiled.

"Then why in the hell do you keep showing up at my homicide scenes?" Miles asked angrily. "You know, they say that the perpetrator always returns to the scene of the crime."

"Are you accusing me of something, Lieutenant?" Josh asked.

"If I was, you'd be in handcuffs," Miles barked back.

"The day you try to slap handcuffs on me is the day you decide that you want to spend a long time in a maximum-security federal penitentiary," Josh warned.

"Sir, we have something," an officer informed the lieutenant.

"What is it?"

"We have a witness who saw a man and a woman fleeing around the back of the motel."

"A man and a woman?" Miles asked.

"Any descriptions?" Ellington chimed in.

The officer shook his head. "No, too dark."

"Any description of a vehicle?" Ellington asked.

Again, the officer shook his head.

"She has a man with her?" Ellington asked.

"We don't even know if it's her," said Davis.

"It's her. But who in the hell is with her?"

"I don't know, but we're running out of time."

"Where would you go if you just left a murder scene?" Ellington asked. "Where would she go that was safe?"

"I don't know, but if I was her, I know where I wouldn't be going. I wouldn't be going to Grandma's, or to her friend Markita's. Remember, she's still got some asshole out searching for her."

"If she's smart, she's on her way out of town. She's got to be; there's nowhere left for her to go. Especially knowing that a maniac is after her," Ellington said. "She's getting out of town tonight."

"Who is this 'she'?" Miles asked.

"It's in the report," Ellington told him. She and Davis raced out of the motel room and headed for their car. "She's going for the money!"

"Yeah, but where?" Davis asked, climbing into the vehicle.

"Where in the hell would you keep that kinda cash?" Ellington asked. "And, remember, wherever it is, it's got to be accessible to her tonight. That pretty much rules out all the banks."

"So, where else do you store money?" Davis asked. He and Ellington stared at each other. The answer hit them both at the same time. "At a fucking storage unit!"

"Call Cleaver!" Ellington told him. "And the lieutenant!" She peeled out of the parking lot.

Neither of them saw the FBI agents in the Chevrolet Impala pull off behind them. And neither was aware that a tracking device had been planted beneath their car.

"What are we doing?" Gena asked, peering out the window.

"What do you mean?" Quadir asked.

"I mean, this, all of this? What are we doing?"

"We're running. What does it look like?"

"I know, I can see that we're running; it's just that I'm trying to figure out where we're going from here."

"Safe, we're going somewhere safe."

"Safe, did you say safe? That's a fucking joke, but then again, I guess I would be safe with you, huh? Now you can call your wolves off, right?"

"Wolves? What are you talking about?"

"Quadir, because of you, my grandmother was brutally raped, Gary is all fucked up and needs more corrective surgery, my friend Markita is dead. She was raped and then killed."

"Hold on, Gena, I didn't have anything to do with what happened to Gah Git or Gary or Markita. Ever since you left, I've been looking for you. I'm putting myself out there rescuing you and all you can do is point the finger at me like I've done something? I saved you from Jerrell, remember? And if I hadn't come when I had, Rik would have had your ass tied up and buried six feet under."

"I thought . . ."

"You thought wrong. I don't know who is behind the attacks on your family. I just figured that whoever it is, he is after my money. Come to think of it, where is my money, Gena? Because I really want it back. I want my money back."

Gena sat and listened with her eyes wide open at every word he spoke. He was telling the truth. He really did have nothing to do with the attacks. *Then who the hell is after me if it's not him?*

"You haven't been after me to get your money back?"

"After you for what? Gena, you're going to give me my

money back. I don't have to harm you or anyone else. I know you're going to give me my money back."

He spoke as if he had a crystal ball foreseeing the future. *Why does he think I'll give him anything? Is he crazy? Does he really think that I would give him all that money so he can go run off with his Doctor Dolittle bitch and have a merry life, while I have nothing? He must be mad. I won't do it.*

Quadir pulled over the car to the side of the road, put it in park, and took his foot off the brake. Raindrops began to drizzle, hitting the windshield with every breath he took.

"What?" Gena asked as she kept her eyes glued out the window, unwilling to face him.

"Gena, I want my money. Had I died, Gena, then you would certainly be the rightful owner of my hidden treasure. But you aren't, and I just need you to do the right thing. I really, really, really need you to do the right thing."

"Or what, Quadir?"

He looked at her strangely. "What do you mean or what?"

"What I said. Or what? If I don't give you back your money and do the right thing, then what?"

Quadir thought for a moment. Ever since they had been together he had done nothing but provide for Gena, take care of Gena, and love Gena. To this day, he still did. He couldn't believe that she was that selfish and that greedy, that she wouldn't willingly give him back his paper.

"Then this is where we say good-bye. You go your way and I go mine."

"Just like that, you'd let me go? You'd let me walk away with your money?"

"You know what, Gena, if I had to hurt you, or do anything outside my character in order to make you return my money, then I wouldn't want it. I want my money; yes, I do. I hustled for that shit, I died for that dough—of course I want my money. But you have it now and I can't make you give it to me. It's not a pawn, it's not an option, it's not a deal. There are no deals here, Gena. You want to give me my money back, fine. You don't want to give me my money back, then all that shows me is that all this time I was completely wrong about you. And if I'm wrong, then I don't want to be right. You take it, have it all, if that's what you want, but I swear to God, you'll never ever have to worry about ever seeing me again. Ever."

He spoke with true conviction in his tone. He wanted to be as forceful as possible without hurting her. He didn't know if she believed him, but every word he spoke was the God's honest truth. If she didn't tell him where his money was, he had every intention of leaving her standing on the side of the road, he had every intention of moving on, even if it meant moving on without her.

She watched as the rain fell and listened to every word he spoke. Deep down, she knew he was right. She also knew that once she gave him the money, she'd probably never see him again. The money was his, all his. It wasn't hers; he was right. And the right thing to do was to let him have it. If that's what he wanted, then she would oblige him and give it back.

"It's at 4-U-Self-Storage," she whispered as she kept her head turned away from him. The last thing she wanted him to see was her tears. The little bit of pride she had was swallowed up by his demands and the reality that she would be left with nothing, not even him.

A DEADLY RINGER

Excuse me, may I help you?" asked the storage night watchman.

"Yes, I'm looking for a storage unit," replied Terrell in all seriousness.

"Oh, we have plenty. What size unit do you need?"

"No, you've already rented the unit I want."

"I'm sorry, come again? I don't understand."

"I'm looking for a storage unit in the name of Gena Scott," said Terrell, hoping and praying this guy was smart enough to just give him the storage unit number.

"I'm not following you," said the guy as he brushed his blond hair back from his forehead.

Just then Terrell noticed a Range Rover pulling into the storage unit. He watched the truck park and noticed the girl and the guy immediately.

"Never mind, thank you."

"I'm sorry, excuse me, you can't go out that doo—"

Terrell silenced the night watchman with a gunshot to the

head. The night watchman slumped down like a cartoon character. Terrell stuffed his body under a desk, placed a sign on
the counter that read BE BACK IN 15 MINUTES, and walked out
the door the night watchman had told him he couldn't use.

Quadir pulled up to the storage facility and parked around
the back. He peered around the nearly empty parking lot and
thought twice about where he was parked. He backed the
Range Rover deep into a wooded area next to the storage facility, parked, and then followed Gena around the various units
until she came upon hers.

Gena led Quadir to her storage room. She used her key to
unlock the lock, opened the door, and showed him the two
suitcases filled with his cash. Quadir rushed over to the suitcases, opened them, and breathed a sigh of relief. His money
was there.

"Let's hurry," he told her.

Quadir lifted the suitcases as they both headed for the door,
only to find a stranger waiting for them.

"Going somewhere?"

*I thought he was dead. Oh, my God, nobody dies anymore?
What's he doing here?* Gena thought to herself, amazed at the
dead man in front of her.

"Jerrell," said Quadir, unsure, and knowing that Jerrell had
died during their altercation in the motel room.

"Naw, nigga, don't look so amazed; you act like you don't
remember me. Nigga, we grew up together."

"Terrell?" asked Quadir, realizing it wasn't Jerrell at all but
his brother, his older twin brother, Terrell.

"That's right, you do remember me. I used to fuck you up
at the playground, nigga. You couldn't hide either, remember?

I'd find you and whoop your little ass and take your fucking lunch money."

"Who is he?" asked Gena, still not connecting the dots.

"He's Jerrell's twin brother, the one that's been after you. He must have thought you killed Jerrell." Quadir added that line with mad sarcasm, hoping to catch Terrell's attention. "Truth is, you should have been after me, Terrell. I'm the one who killed your brother, not her. And all that talk about the playground, just know it's a new day, nigga, and I'll murk your ass just like I buried your brother."

Ice-cold blood ran through Terrell's veins at the sound of Quadir voice. He stood toe to toe with Quadir. Their eyes met and Terrell saw no remorse. Quadir's face was emotionless. He had no sympathy and no regard for what he had done and to top it all off, he had the nerve to admit that it was he who had in fact murdered his brother, without fear, at that. *Who do this nigga think he is? Him and this bird-ass broad. I'm going to fuck her while he watches. We'll see how cocky this motherfucker is then.*

Quadir saw the gun first, and he reacted. He slung one of the suitcases toward Terrell, distracting him. Terrell caught the bag as Quadir dove into him, knocking the gun away and sending it sliding down the hall. The two of them fell to the floor and began to struggle. Gena knew that it was him. She knew that this had to be the man who had brutally violated her grandmother, the man who shot Gary, the man who shot Bria's boyfriend, the man who killed Markita. And now she knew why. He looked just like his fucking brother; he looked just like Jerrell. He had been stalking her to avenge his brother's death.

Terrell and Quadir grappled with each other, rolling around

on the floor, jockeying for position while trying to free their hands. Each was occupied with not allowing the other's hands to become free. Both men knew that they were in a life-and-death struggle.

Terrell threw a punch that landed squarely on Quadir's jaw that stunned him and allowed Terrell to throw Quadir off him. He immediately began to crawl for his weapon. Quadir grabbed Terrell's leg and yanked him back. He punched Terrell in his back and side and crawled back on top of him. Terrell elbowed Quadir in his stomach and rolled over, again knocking Quadir off him. Quadir threw a wild punch, striking Terrell in his chin. He followed that with a left cross that struck Terrell's nose. Terrell swung and landed a solid blow on the side of Quadir's head. This blow was followed by one that landed on Quadir's ear. Quadir wrapped his hands around Terrell's throat, determined to squeeze the life out of him. Terrell broke Quadir's grasp by kneeing him in his testicles. Pain shot through Quadir's body, causing him to cry out.

Quadir's wounds had closed, but they had not fully healed. His tissue began to pull apart from the inside, causing a searing pain throughout his body. He knew that he wasn't going to last much longer, not going blow for blow with the monster he was battling. But, then again, he knew that he couldn't lose. His life and Gena's life were on the line. Not to mention that if he ended up at another crime scene, Amelia's life too would be affected, and he didn't want that. If his body were found, there would be some serious consequences behind it. Amelia would lose her license and probably even go to jail. Gena would lose her life, and that would definitely send her grandmother to an early grave. So many people depended on him at that moment. So many people were counting on him to be the man they always believed him to be. Was he truly gangsta? Was he really built to last? Were they all wrong for looking up to him, admiring him, wanting to be like him?

Quadir summoned every piece of strength that he had left in his body and swung at Terrell. The blow sounded as though it could be heard clear across the city. He followed it with another blow, and then another. He wanted to put this nigga to sleep. But Terrell had other plans.

Terrell growled and head-butted Quadir, opening a gash between Quadir's eyes, just above his nose. Terrell knew that he was built to last. He wasn't going out like no sucker. He wrapped his hands around Quadir's throat.

Gena could hear Quadir gasping for air. She raced down the dark hallway searching for Terrell's gun. Desperate, she dropped to her knees and scoured the floor until she found it. Quadir needed her. And despite what she had said before, she didn't want him to die. She loved him. She wanted him to live. She needed him to live. No matter what happened between them, no matter what was going to happen between them in the future, she wanted him to live, even if that meant he'd be with someone else.

Gena raced back to where Quadir and Terrell were struggling and pointed the gun. She was scared to pull the trigger. Scared of hitting Quadir instead of Terrell. Scared of actually having to kill another human being.

Quadir's eyes rolled to the back of his head and slowly he leaned forward. Terrell smiled, knowing that he was squeezing the life out of Quadir. There was nothing like killing a person with one's bare hands. Quadir leaned forward until his and Terrell's faces were nearly touching. And then he smiled. He was a built-to-last nigga.

Quadir opened his mouth and clamped down on Terrell's nose with the ferocity of a hungry pit bull. He shifted his last bit of energy to his jaw muscles and bit until his teeth met. Blood ran down his chin as he rose and spat Terrell's nose down the hallway. Terrell covered the bloody hole where his nose used to be and rolled around on the floor screaming in pain.

Quadir kicked Terrell in the head, then stomped his head down into the ground so that the back of it hit the concrete floor hard. He stomped again, and again, and then again. After the fourth stomp, blood oozed from the back of Terrell's head, and he stopped moving completely. Quadir turned to Gena, who rushed into his arms.

Quadir was barely able to stand. His old wounds felt as though someone were sticking a red-hot poker into his flesh. He was out of breath, tired, and sore all at once. "Help me pick up all of the money," he said weakly. "We got to get out of here."

Dick Davis hung up his cell phone and turned to his partner. "Ratzinger said that this thing's getting out of hand. He wants us to tighten things up."

Ellington peered over at her partner. He looked pale.

"Dickie, what's the matter?"

"He wants us to kill her," Davis whispered. "He wants us to kill her and whoever's with her. No witnesses."

Ellington nodded. She had known what the deal was from the beginning. She knew that Gena's death warrant had been signed the moment they all agreed to go after that money. Davis was green. "Dickie, are you okay on this?"

Davis nodded. He hadn't bargained on having to kill anyone. He thought it would be just a matter of taking some drug money away from some undeserving little dope dealer's wife and distributing it among police officers who truly deserved it. But murdering people over it, that was something else entirely. Would that make them worse than the drug dealers?

"What did Cleaver say?" Ellington asked.

"He said that there's only one self-storage place along this highway that is open this late. That's 4-U-Self Storage."

"He give you an address?"

"Yeah."

"Well, let's go and get our fucking money," Ellington said excitedly.

"Josh, it's Steve over in technical," Lavon Stokes said.

"Hi, Steve!" Josh shouted toward the receiver.

"Josh says hi, Steve." Lavon told him. She turned back to Josh. "Steve says that they just intercepted a call from Ratzinger, giving the order to kill the girl."

"Holy shit! They got it on tape again?"

Lavon nodded. "He says that he's already played the tape for Galvani, who had it played for the district attorney and for one of the federal magistrates. The judge is heading into his office to sign the arrest warrants as we speak."

"Yes!"

"The district attorney is going before the grand jury first thing in the morning with evidence," Lavon told him.

Phil patted Josh on his shoulder. "Good work."

"Ask Steve where those assholes are right now. I want to slap the cuffs on them as soon as the warrants are signed," Josh said.

"Steve, you got a location on the suspects' vehicles?" Lavon asked. She turned back to Josh. "Cleaver's vehicle is headed this way. Ellington's car is just up ahead. Ratzinger is still at the station."

"Good work, Steve!" Josh shouted toward the handset. "Get rid of Steve, and call Tony, Mike, and Dan. Have Tony and Mike round up Ratzinger, and tell Dan to meet up with us as soon as we give him a location. We can take down Cleaver, Ellington, and Davis all at once. Get me some more agents out here. We're going to get these sons of bitches tonight!"

THE GETAWAY

Ellington pulled up about the time Cleaver arrived.

"Are you sure this is the place?" Cleaver asked. "I hope that I don't look like an asshole."

"What's with the patrol cars?" Ellington whispered.

Cleaver shook his head. "I sent them. That little bitch isn't giving us the slip this time. There's a fire escape around the back of the building. I'm going to send the officers in through the front, while we are going to go and cover the back, which is probably how they intend to escape."

Davis nodded. "Good thinking."

"Ready to get paid?" Cleaver asked with a smile.

A gun went off inside the building, causing several of the gathered officers to duck and scatter for cover.

Several black Suburbans raced into the parking lot. Josh, Phil, and Lavon leaped out of the lead SUV and rushed up to Ellington, Davis, and Cleaver.

"Nice night for an arrest, isn't it?" Cleaver smiled.

Josh smiled and shook his head. "You took the words right outta my mouth, you sack of shit."

"Turn around and place your hands on your heads!" Lavon shouted.

"What?" Ellington asked.

"We're fucking cops, you assholes!" Cleaver protested.

Phil and several other agents had their weapons drawn.

"I said turn around and put your hands over your heads!" Lavon shouted again.

"This is bullshit!" Ellington said. She turned and placed her hands over her head. Davis did the same.

"Turn around and place your hands on your head!" Josh told Cleaver.

"Will you wait just a goddamned minute!" Cleaver shouted. "I am Internal Affairs, and you're interfering in some serious police business!"

"I'm FBI, and I say you have no business being a police officer!" Josh told him. "Now stop resisting, before I have Phil shoot you!"

"We have suspects inside!" Cleaver shouted. "And a damn gun just went off!"

"The real cops will take care of it!" Josh told him. "Now turn around!"

"You fucking asshole! They're escaping around the back!" Cleaver shouted.

Josh drew his weapon.

"You going to let them fucking escape!" Cleaver shouted. He pulled away from Josh and began running.

Josh holstered his pistol and chased Cleaver, tackling him by the side of the building. The other agents quickly came to

Josh's assistance. They manhandled Cleaver into submission and handcuffed him.

"They're getting away!" Cleaver shouted. "Agent, let me talk to you in private! I have a deal for you that you can't resist!"

Josh turned to Phil. "Go and listen to his deal, and then add attempting to bribe a federal agent to his charges."

Phil laughed and headed off to the SUV, where the other agents were shoving Cleaver inside. Lavon walked up to Josh.

"And what are we going to do about them?" she asked, nodding toward the storage facility.

Josh shrugged. "Not our business, Lavon. Not our business. We're here to bust some crooked cops."

Lavon lifted an eyebrow. "There's a lot of money in there that somebody is getting away with."

"It's her money, and judging from the things that have happened to her, she deserves it. Hey, Lavon, I get my jollies fucking over the big guy, not the little ones." Josh walked to the front of the building and stared up at it. "You better run, girl. And you better take that money, and you better do something with it. Do something good with it."

A patrolman walked out of the storage unit building.

"Find anything?" Josh asked.

"Two bodies. The night clerk and an unidentified black man," the officer told him.

"Anybody else?"

The officer shook his head. "No, sir."

"Call Detective Curtis Miles from Homicide," Josh told the officer. "Tell him that in all probability, I've got the murder suspect that he's been searching for lying dead in there."

The officer nodded and headed for his patrol car.

"Wow, we saved the day, huh?" Lavon asked.

"We sure did. Good work, agent," Josh told her. He pulled her close and wrapped his arm around her. "C'mon, let's get outta here. Buy you a hot cup of coffee."

"And a doughnut?" Lavon asked, as if the coffee just wasn't enough.

"Sprinkles?"

"Yeah, sprinkles."

AND THAT'S ALL, FOLKS

One Year Later

The water was absolutely postcard perfect. It looked as though someone had clicked a button on a computer and chosen the perfect color blue for a brochure ad. Royal blue faded into aquamarine see-through water, breathtaking, simply beautiful, just a few shades darker than the cloudless baby-blue sky sitting above it. Gena couldn't believe she was back where it all started: The Valiant Hotel on Paradise Island in the Grand Bahamas.

Palm trees swayed gently in the soft breeze, moderating the temperate Caribbean climate even more. The weather was a perfect seventy-seven degrees, while beneath the white silk canopies it felt as though it was no higher than seventy.

All of the guests were dressed in white. The women wore white cotton beach gowns, while the gentlemen all wore white cotton shirts and pants. All of the guests wore sandals, as the ceremony was being held on the white-sand beach. White gardenia floral arrangements were arrayed around the canopy and the tables and chairs beneath it. Eighteen white doves that had been imported from Europe sat in cages around the beach, waiting to be released at the conclusion of the nuptials.

Gena sat alone in a small dressing room. Everything was perfect, there was no detail left unfinished, nothing more to do. The day had dawned with a perfect, sunny, cloudless sky, and who could ask for more? Gena thought back to the night she met Quadir in Harlem on 125th Street in front of the Mart 125. Who could have known; who could have guessed? They had been through the fire together and had made it without getting burned.

A gentle knock at the door brought Gena out of her reverie.

"Come in," she said as she watched a tall, handsome man, wearing a tuxedo and looking like a million bucks, stick his head around the door. "Daddy, come here, Daddy," said Gena, her arms reaching out for the father she had never known.

"You look like a princess," Malcolm said, his eyes beginning to water. "I don't know if I can do this, Gena, all those people out there and all."

"Daddy, you'll be fine; I'm going to hold your hand and we're going to walk together just like we did last night at rehearsal." Gena smiled reassuringly.

"I wish your mama could see you," said Malcolm, seeing his wife in his daughter's smile.

"I know, Dad, I know. Listen . . ." said Gena, taking her father's hands into her own and staring up into his big strong brown eyes. "We can't change the past, but we can change where we go from here, from now on. It's okay. My mother's not here; the only thing that matters to me is that . . . you are, you're here. And I'm so, so grateful for this day."

"Baby girl, you think you're grateful. Them white folks had me locked up so long, I don't know if I'm coming or going, and I know that I don't have much . . ." Malcolm stopped for a minute, to clear his throat, "but I'd give my life for you, Gena, I'd give my right arm for you to have this day."

"Oh, Daddy, I love you," she said, embracing her father.

"I love you too, baby girl; I love you too."

"Hey, whatch'all doin' in here?" asked Michael, peeking through the partially open door. "Wow, Gena, look at you. You must be the most beautiful bride I ever laid my two eyes on."

"She sure is," said Malcolm.

"Uncle Michael," said Gena, running over to her uncle.

"It's been a rough couple of years, but you weathered the storm. You and Quadir have nothing but smooth seas ahead," he said, with his hands firmly on Gena's shoulder. "I pray God blesses your union today and for the rest of your lives," said Michael, congratulating her.

"Oh, Uncle Michael, you're going to make me cry too. Look, my makeup, y'all," said Gena, making her way over to the mirror for one last glance.

"You okay, brother man," said Michael gripping his older brother's hand and hugging him.

"Yeah, I'm here. I don't know what I'm doing, but I'm here."

"Hey, don't worry; I got you, man," said Michael.

"Seriously, though, I think I need to take you up on that offer. I can't walk her down this aisle, man."

Michael looked at his brother and then down at his watch, "Okay, guys, let's go, let's make time."

Holding a bouquet of white roses in her hand, Gena stepped

out into the hallway and found her wedding party all lined up, waiting and ready to make that walk.

Everybody was there, not one person had been left out. Viola walked over to Gena and kissed the side of her face.

"I don't think I've ever seen a more beautiful bride."

"Thank you, Viola, for everything."

Viola lined up the wedding party, nodded with approval toward Gena, and gave the cue for the music to begin. The groomsmen and the bridesmaids took their places at the altar; the flower girls and the tiny ring bearer walked down the red carpet next. Viola took her seat next to Montel and her daughter, Denise, just as the bride appeared at the doorway.

"Aaaww," was all that could be heard as everyone turned around to see Malcolm standing tall and proud on her left and Michael standing tall and proud on her right. Everyone there knew about the situation between the two brothers, the death of Gena's mother, the reasons of it all, and even Gena's questionable paternity, but on this day, none of that mattered. The only thing that mattered was that they were all there together. But for Gah Git to see both her boys standing side by side after being separated for so, so long, brought tears to her eyes. She didn't know what she was crying for, but she couldn't stop.

"Gah Git, you okay?" asked Paula.

"She all right. She just crying at the sight of Malcolm and Michael holding Gena," said Gwendolyn, grabbing a tissue out of a crying Royce's hand and handing it to Paula to pass to Gah Git.

"Give me my tissue back, woman," Royce demanded.

"Fool, don't start wit' me on this goddamn island out here

in the middle of nowhere," Gwendolyn whispered harshly at him as she passed the tissue to her sister.

"It's been used," said Paula, frowning.

"So, it ain't gonna kill her," said Gwendolyn, shoving the tissue back at Paula.

Gena, her father, and her uncle made their way down the aisle.

"Dag, Uncle Malcolm look good, right?" whispered Brianna.

"Mmm-hmm, real good, he looks better than Uncle Michael," whispered Bria back to her twin.

"I see why Gena's mom was dickin' 'em both down, now."

"Mmm-hmm, she sure was," added Bria, as Gena's two bridesmaids snickered to each other throughout the entire ceremony.

Gena looked as if she belonged in a Walt Disney World parade. She glowed like a real fairy tale princess wearing Cinderella's gown about to finally kiss her Prince Charming for everyone to bear witness to.

A Caribbean band played the traditional wedding march as she made her way to her floral altar. Only the minister was wearing black. When they finally reached the end of their walk, her uncle Michael reached down and kissed her cheek before stepping to the side. It was Malcolm who then placed his daughter's hand into Quadir's. He looked at her father, and the two men nodded at each other with approval. Holding hands, Quadir and Gena faced each other.

"Dearly beloved, we are gathered here today to join together these two young people in holy matrimony."

But the moment of all moments was when a tiny Quanda stepped forward and handed Quadir a red-and-gold Cartier box containing their wedding bands. It was probably the sweetest gesture of the ceremony.

"Thanks, baby girl," said Quadir, as he bent and took the box out of his Quanda's hands.

"I now pronounce you husband and wife. You may kiss the bride."

DISCUSSION QUESTIONS

1. Did you think Quadir's explanation for faking his death was believable?

2. Should Gena have understood why he lied?

3. Do you think Gena should have understood Quadir's relationship with Amelia? What about Quadir understanding Gena's relationship with Jerrell?

4. What are your thoughts on the attack on Gah Git? Markita?

5. Did you think Terrell was crazier than his brother Jerrell?

6. Would the police have schemed to take someone's money—as they did Gena's drug money—in real life?

7. Are you glad the police were caught?

8. Do you think it was good that Quadir and Gena got away with the money?

9. Are you glad they got together in the end?

10. Did you think it was good that Gena's father came home?

11. Did you want to know more about Gena and her family?

12. Do you think it was fair for Aunt Gwendolyn to blame Gena for what happened to Gah Git?

13. Do you think Markita should have been more careful when Terrell confronted her at her apartment?

14. Would you have thought that Rik would have turned against Gena? Quadir?

15. What are your thoughts about Quadir killing Rik?

New York Times bestselling author
TERI WOODS
brings you back
to the hard streets of Philadelphia . . .

Please turn this page
for a preview of

ALIBI

Coming in 2009 from
Grand Central Publishing

CHAPTER ONE

1986

H ey, Lance, come here, look," whispered Jeremy, standing in an alleyway and pointing to a window in what appeared to be an apartment row house on the 2500 block of Somerset Street in North Philadelphia.

"What? I don't see nothing," whispered Lance back to him.

"The window—it's cracked. It's not shut all the way. Right there. You see it?" asked Jeremy, as he pointed to the window showing Lance his keen eye vision.

"You sure they in there?" Lance asked, trying to figure out what the next move should be as an alley cat jumped out of a tree, scaring the living daylights out of him.

"Nigga, I know you not laughing."

"Naw, for real though, I'm telling you, I followed them all day. They in there. I watched them go in there with two duffel bags. They went in and they haven't come out, neither one of them. And them duffel bags they had were chunky, real chunky. They holding a lot of money or a lot of coke."

So many different thoughts rushed around in Lance's head. The first one being how much money and how much coke their rival competition was holding in the house. Right now, more than ever, he needed a come up. A strong come up and he knew in his heart that this was it.

"You sure it's just the two of them in there?" Lance asked again, his heart starting to beat a little faster as the adrenaline rushed throughout his veins.

"Man, I'm telling you. We can take these jokers. They caught off guard; they won't even see us coming. We got one chance, Lance, just one, and this is it."

Lance needed to play the whole scene out in his head. He wanted no stone to be left unturned. There could be no mistakes, no mishaps, and no time for fuck-ups. Jeremy might be right; this just might be his one and only chance or, better yet, his golden opportunity to come up. Times were hard and the only nigga in the city moving weight was Simon Shuller. Simon Shuller had been getting money for years. Everyone knew it too. Not only was he the largest drug dealer in Philadelphia, he had to be the police as well. There was no way he could run drugs, dope, and numbers year after year and not be in jail by now. But he wasn't in jail and Simon Shuller, police or not, was the man with the golden hand in the city. The big kahuna with all the money and those two unknown suspects inside the row home on Somerset were his runners. Truth was they could have left the door wide open, 'cause anybody crazy enough to mess with anything belonging to Simon Shuller had to be plumb out of their minds.

"Man, I must be crazy listening to you," said Lance, as he looked at Jeremy.

"Shit, you crazy if you don't, my friend. I'm telling you, we might not ever get this chance in life again. We could sneak in, take what we came for, and sneak right back out."

Lance thought for a minute longer. *Maybe Jeremy is right. We sneak in, take what we came for, and sneak back out. How hard could that be?*

"Okay, come on, let's do the damn thing," Lance commanded, feeling nothing but heart.

"That's what I'm talking about, baby boy. Don't worry, I got this caper all figured out already. Come on, let's get the car and park it close enough to make our getaway."

Up on the fire escape, Lance looked at Jeremy, who was silently cracking the window open. He turned around and waved his hand for his friend to come on. He climbed through the window and into what once may have been a bathroom. Jeremy turned around to find Lance on the fire escape climbing through the window behind him.

"What the fuck died in this motherfucker?" whispered Lance, as a foul stench in the air filled his nostrils.

"Sshh, come on," said Jeremy as he embraced his 9mm and peeked around the corner of the doorway looking like he belonged on the force.

What the fuck do this nigga think he doing?

"What? Why you looking at me like that?"

"Nigga, you ain't no goddamn Barnaby Jones and shit. What is you doing?"

"I'm trying to make sure the coast is clear, man. Let me do what I do," said Jeremy, a tad bit annoyed.

Between the two of them whispering back and forth, neither of them heard the footsteps coming down the hallway. Not until the footsteps were right on them and the bathroom door came flying open.

"What the fuck? Ya'll niggas lost?" said a tall, brown-skinned fellow, wearing a Phillies jacket and Phillies baseball cap.

At first he thought they might've been crackheads, but then he saw the shiny chrome and knew differently.

"Shut the fuck up, before I kill you in this motherfucker," said Jeremy, as he quickly maneuvered his gun and pointed it straight at his victim's head. "Come on, let's go."

Jeremy held the man on his left side, close to his body. He held his gun in his right hand up to the man's head; they began walking back down the hallway as they heard another guy calling from the living room.

"Yo, Ponch, we need more vials. You gonna have to run down to the . . ."

His sentence was cut short as he saw his man, Poncho, being led by Jeremy and Lance through the doorway with a gun to his head.

"Don't even think about it, shorty," said Lance, as he pointed his gun at the guy sitting at the table stuffing tiny vials with two hits of crack.

"What the fuck?"

"Nigga, you know what it is. Bag that shit up, put it back in the duffel bag and don't nobody got to get hurt."

Nard quickly surveyed everything that was going on. *These dudes ain't wearing no masks. That can only mean one thing.* And even though Jeremy and Lance's intention wasn't to kill, just rob, Nard felt otherwise, and being a true thoroughbred for Simon Shuller he'd rather die fighting than give them niggas a dime, even if the coke wasn't his. Some things in life were just more important, and his reputation for being a "real nigga" was one of them. Nard was a young man, but for the dough, he had love. For the streets, he had respect, and for a principle about some bullshit, he would fight tooth and nail. He reached under the table he was sitting at and felt for his gun, which he always kept duct-taped to the bottom. Quickly, his fingers fondled it until his grasp was tight. Nard came from under the table so fast, no one saw it coming, not even Poncho. He shot Lance one time in the chest, the bullet piercing his heart. Lance dropped to the floor, holding his chest in one hand and his gun in the other. He looked up at Jeremy gasping for breath and collapsing in a red pool of blood.

"Let him go, motherfucker!" shouted Nard.

"Nard, take this nigga. Take him. I know you can, baby boy, take him," Poncho yelled.

"Shut up, shut the fuck up," said Jeremy, now nervous as his man was gasping for air, gurgling blood, and reaching for him to help him.

"Let him go, let him go. Let him go and I'll let you live," said Nard, meaning every word he spoke.

"Nigga, give me what the fuck I came for or both you motherfuckers is gonna die," said Jeremy with lots of heart, as he used brute force and pushed the gun harder into the side of Poncho's head. He looked down on the floor. Lance was dead.

"Motherfucker, I ain't giving you shit. Let him go!" Nard yelled again.

"Take him, Nard. What the fuck is you waiting fo . . ."

The gunshot seemed unreal at first, a mistake, a misfortune, something that wasn't suppose to be, a gap, a space, time that needed to rewind. Slow motion, so slow as Jeremy felt Poncho's body slump to the floor as Nard watched Poncho, his main man, die right in front him. Poncho's blood, and fragments of his head, landed on Nard all within a matter of seconds.

Instinct moved through Nard, like a thief in the night and like lightning. The strike of the bullet that hit Jeremy's chest threw him back against the door. He dropped his gun and looked down at the blood pouring out his body. Jeremy didn't even see it coming—it just happened so fast. Nard hit him with the strike of magic, and poof, just like that, Jeremy was gone.

"Fuck!" yelled Nard, as he held his head in his right hand, his gun still in his left. "Fuck, goddamn it. Fuck you come here for, stupid ass motherfuckers?" he yelled, as he angrily interrogated a dead Jeremy and a dead Lance. "Damn, what the fuck am I gonna do now?"

He surveyed the room, as he talked and cursed the dead bodies around him. "Motherfuckers!" he said as he kicked a lifeless Jeremy. He checked the three bodies laying on the floor for a pulse, starting with his man, Poncho.

"Damn, Ponch, man. I'm sorry, man. I'm sorry," he said, as he felt Poncho's wrist. "I love you, man. I love you. Fuck!" He started thinking about the consequences of what had just happened. "Fucking police, man. Fuck, what am I going to do?"

He just couldn't think straight. His brain was overwhelmed to say the least. He threw the crack and vials and other paraphernalia in a red duffel bag, and left the other duffel bag, which was empty lying on the floor. He looked around the room, grabbed all the contents that belonged to him, tried to wipe off the table, doorknobs, and everything else he had touched in the crack spot and quickly ran out the door and down a flight of stairs.

"Hey Nard, be careful, they shooting in the building."

He quickly turned around, his gun still in his hand, but tucked inside the front pocket of his hoodie.

"Hey, shorty," he said, as he looked at a kid standing in the vestibule. He couldn't have been more than nine maybe ten years old. He didn't know the kid's name, but this kid always knew his. "Yeah, you be careful too, kid."

He quickly brushed past him, threw his hoodie over his head and made his way out the door as he quickly walked down the street to his car.

"DaShawn, get in here! Don't you hear them shooting? Come on, boy!"

Nard looked up and saw a young black girl hanging out a

window, hollering for the same young kid that Nard had just brushed past.

Please tell me this little young kid or the window chick ain't no problem. Fuck, man, fuck! I need me an alibi. And where the fuck is Sticks? Simon is gonna be heated, but at least I got his coke. That's all I need to do is get at Simon. I got to get rid of this gun, too. Yeah, that's all I'll need is an alibi and I'm good.